BETWEEN THE MOON AND THE ROCK

Judy Allen

RED FOX

A Red Fox Book

Published by Random House Children's Books
20 Vauxhall Bridge Road, London SW1V 2SA

A division of Random House UK Ltd
London Melbourne Sydney Auckland
Johannesburg and agencies throughout the world

© Judy Allen 1992

First published by Julia MacRae 1992
Red Fox edition 1994

1 3 5 7 9 10 8 6 4 2

Printed and bound in Great Britain by
Cox & Wyman Ltd, Reading, Berkshire

RANDOM HOUSE UK Limited Reg. No. 954009

ISBN 0 09 918651 9

· CHAPTER ONE ·

IN THE LIGHT and easy days, before any of them were aware of the dark energies building up, Mother Grundy and Lisa often walked through bandit-country at the end of the afternoon. That was how Flora knew where to find them when it was time to plant the tree.

Bandit-country was safe enough in daylight. It stretched between the end of the town on the one side and the beginning of the country on the other, and it gave sanctuary to all the things that didn't belong in either – the allotments, the town dump, the cemetery.

The road ran confidently straight as far as the brightly painted fence that surrounded the dump. Then it curved to the right and headed for the distant clump of trees that marked the cemetery. Here, rather aptly, it came to a dead-end.

Way beyond the allotments ran the disused railway line. Beside the track stood a derelict hut where shadowy groups met on pre-arranged nights and sniffed things, and bought and sold things, and were occasionally cornered by the headlights of prowling police cars.

Lisa walked slowly past the allotments, bored but not minding being bored, scuffing through the little dun-coloured pebbles that lay among the clumps of rough grass at the edge of the road. Once, she stopped to turn over the cassette in her Walkman. She had picked up the wrong tape

1

on the way out of the house, an old one she was sick of, but she played it through anyway, for want of anything else to listen to. She was vaguely aware of the little crooked brown allotment sheds, the avenues of bean poles, the shaggy compost heaps, but she didn't pay any attention to them. The old labrador plodded ahead, stopping often to examine things on the ground.

Flora said that Lisa spent most of her time in a dream, and in a way she was right. But it was a bland sort of dream, without detail or drama, an unfocused drifting dream. Mostly, Lisa wasn't really seeing what she was looking at and wasn't really thinking about what was passing through her mind.

There was a fence between bandit-country and the town, but it had no gate, just an enormous opening, wide enough for a hearse to pass a pick-up truck. It was from this opening that Flora saw them, just as they reached the end of the final allotment and turned to come back. Mother Grundy was too slow and stiff to want to go further, and Lisa was content to let her set the pace.

Flora waved and began to run.

If Flora, too, lived in a dream, then hers was a vivid lively one, and she drew everything around her into her dream with her. Flora's dream didn't deaden or block reality, it woke it up and sharpened it. She ran towards the distant figures through a jewelled landscape. The October sun was low in the sky and its rich light was making diamonds of the tiny bits of quartz in the road surface, and finding emeralds in the stagnant water caught in a dip in an empty fertiliser bag.

As she ran, little glittering stones flying, she saw the sudden clumps of dahlias that blazed red and yellow among the blue-green winter cabbages, and she heard the carrion crows raging in the cemetery trees as waves of starlings swept in from the south, rested briefly, then swirled on to the town centre and the civic buildings where they chose to spend the night.

Lisa saw her and pulled out the ear-pieces of the Walkman.

"I've come to get you," called Flora, as she got nearer. "Today's the day! Mum brought the tree back with her just now."

Lisa smiled – then she frowned across at the cemetery. "You've annoyed the birds," she said. "Listen to the row they're making."

Later, much later, she said that she'd noticed there were more crows this year than before, more foxes, more magpies – bandits and outlaws, every one – and that she had taken their increase to be some kind of warning. However, although she believed this, it wasn't true. It was Flora who noticed things, and understood them. Even when Flora pointed them out to her Lisa didn't always see them, or not in the way Flora did.

"The crows shriek every evening," said Flora. "You'd know if you didn't always have your ears plugged up. Come on."

"In a second," said Lisa, "Mother Grundy's found something interesting in the shrubbery." Only for Mother Grundy would Lisa ever ask Flora to wait.

Flora bent down, took hold of the labrador's tail and pulled her, very gently, out from under the Michaelmas daisies that bristled through the fence. "You should call her Goldie again," she said. "Why don't you?"

"Dad calls her Old Mother Grundy now she's stout," said Lisa. "He says she likes it because it has more character than 'Goldie'."

"I don't think she likes it," said Flora, nose to nose with the dog, scratching the golden ears until the long tail beat against the fence. "She wants to be the Princess, not the Dame."

"She should worry," said Lisa. "He calls me Chunky."

3

"Don't answer to it," said Flora. "I wouldn't."

Lisa giggled. "I can't imagine anyone calling you anything rude," she said. "I wonder why I'm not jealous of you."

"Nothing to be jealous of," said Flora. "It's all in the mind. You have to keep thinking that you're the way you're meant to be."

"It would help if other people thought so too," said Lisa.

The dog plodded between them, back towards the fence opening, her tail up and moving from side to side as she walked.

"Should we be going faster?" said Lisa. "I don't want to miss anything."

"With any luck Jack and Mum will have dug the hole by the time we get back," said Flora. "But they won't plant the tree without us."

The first two houses beyond the fence opening were large and old. They had been new when the area was a village, before the town grew and claimed it, before the railway track was laid, before the fields went out like the tide – and, unlike the tide, stayed out. In fact anyone who looked carefully could see exactly what was left of the original village. As well as the two houses there was also the little church, its spire only just higher than the modern block of flats beside it, and The Green Man pub beyond that.

Flora lived in the second of the two big houses. Lisa lived next door on the other side, in a small modern house. This arrangement struck both of them as entirely suitable, though neither of them could quite have explained why.

The low sun was still strong enough to warm brick and stone. The air smelt of late roses and the last lawn-trim before the winter rains.

"Do you think they still haunt it?" said Flora, dreamily.

"Who?" said Lisa, startled.

"The first villagers," said Flora.

"They must hate it if they do," said Lisa. "They'd expect

4

a lane with blackberries, not a road with lorries thundering down it to the tip."

"They wouldn't see all that," said Flora comfortably. "They'd see it as it was in their day. They'd walk right through the trucks, give the drivers a hell of a fright."

"I don't believe in ghosts," said Lisa, rather regretfully.

"The pub has a ghost," said Flora, with relish. "In the old bit, at the top of the stairs. A woman who isn't there carries a tray into one of the bedrooms – *without opening the door!*"

Lisa laughed.

"You're not supposed to laugh," said Flora mildly, "you're supposed to shake with terror."

"Your ghosts aren't frightening," said Lisa. "They just sound like ordinary people behaving a bit strangely."

"I think they mostly are," said Flora. "I think they're ordinary people who've lost their way. And their physical bodies, too, of course. Hey, look at *that!*"

Outside the big old house next to Flora's stood a long, low, gleaming American car, all fins and cream upholstery.

"This wasn't here when I came out to get you," said Flora admiringly.

"The new neighbours?" said Lisa. "Who *are* the new neighbours?"

"No idea," said Flora. "People who like big cars, at a guess."

"It seems odd," said Lisa, "them moving into Mrs Paxton's house. As though they're trespassing."

"No, it's all right," said Flora. "She isn't there any more."

"I know *that*," said Lisa. "We went to the funeral! We're planting the tree!" She spoke crossly because there was an image she didn't want to allow back into her mind.

"Yes, but I mean she *really* isn't there any more," said Flora, who was aware of the memory Lisa carried. "I'm sure she knew how to die properly. She'll have gone wherever you're meant to go, she won't be hanging around, walking through walls and resenting the living."

She pushed open her front gate. As she went through it, Lisa, just behind her, saw something that made her stop and stare.

"Flora!" she said. "Your *hair!*"

"What's the matter with it?" said Flora.

"Well," said Lisa, beginning to doubt herself, "it's meant to be yellow, right?"

"Blonde," said Flora, mimicking the mincing stride of a model on a catwalk. "Blonde, *please.*"

"But when the sun shines on it," said Lisa, "like now, I can see green in it. You know, like in some paintings where they do everything the wrong colour and you wonder why. Flora, you have *green* hair."

"Of course," said Flora. "Today is a green day. All its energies are green. We're even having green food later – green pasta, green salad and pistachio ice-cream, with grapes. It's in honour of the tree."

She moved on into the shadow thrown by the house and her long, shiny hair went back to normal.

"Have you put colour on it?" said Lisa. "It doesn't show now."

"Of course not!" said Flora. "It often looks green – you just haven't noticed before. The basic colour of all blonde hair is green. Brown hair is basically red and black hair is blue. Everyone knows that."

"I didn't know that," said Lisa.

"Oh you," said Flora, laughing. "You just don't pay attention." She opened her front door. "Aren't you coming in?"

"In a minute, I have to take Mother Grundy home."

"Come through our house. Hop over the fence like you usually do."

"Mother Grundy's hopping days are over," said Lisa.

"It's because of what you call her," said Flora, and she almost looked cross. "There's magic in names, you know."

Lisa smiled down at the dog.

"You'd better believe me," said Flora. "People with green hair understand these things."

· CHAPTER TWO ·

LISA CALLED OUT as she went through the house, but no one was home yet. While Mother Grundy drank noisily from her bowl, slopping great gouts of water over the edges, Lisa sat at the kitchen table and wrote a note.

'Gone next door,' she wrote, 'to plant Mrs Paxton's tree.'

She watched as the dog climbed into her basket, beside the boiler, turned round twice and flopped down with a comfortable groan.

Lisa turned back to her note. 'I think I'm eating with them,' she wrote.

She stood up to go to the kitchen door, hesitated, and looked down towards her feet. She could see where the denim skirt curved out slightly, across her stomach, and again at the fronts of her thighs. She picked at the waist-band for a moment, then tried to slide just one finger down inside it. It wasn't possible.

She picked up the pencil again and wrote, in the largest lettering there was room for, 'I WON'T EAT TOO MUCH.'

Then she joined Flora, and Flora's mother Katherine, and Flora's grandmother, and her brother Jack, in the next-door garden.

"Hey, Mum," said Flora, "Lisa saw green in my aura just now."

She had to raise her voice against the noise that was coming from Mrs Paxton's old house, where people seemed to be banging furniture about, and hammering, and calling out to each other from all the rooms at once.

Katherine reached out and gave Lisa a quick hug. She smelt faintly of spice and roses and her amber bracelets collided on her arm with a comfortable clunking that Lisa felt rather than heard.

Grandma, who rarely bothered to speak these days, smiled.

"I didn't really see her aura," Lisa confessed to Katherine. "It was just the sun on her hair."

"Where's Goldie?" said Katherine. "Have you left her alone?"

"She's asleep," said Lisa. "She sleeps all the time now she's old." She glanced quickly at Grandma and her cheeks began to glow pinkly. "And fat," she said quickly. "Fat, like me." She picked at her waistband to demonstrate.

"You're not fat," said Katherine, "your skirt's too small."

"Come on! Come on!" said Jack, seizing the flimsy branches of the new tree and shaking them. "Let's *plant* it!"

The hole, as Flora had hoped, was ready – dug, thoroughly watered and waiting, close to the remains of the fence that divided Flora's garden from the tangled wilderness Mrs Paxton had enjoyed neglecting.

The fence had blown down in a winter gale when Jack was only a year old, and no one had seen much point in setting it up again. Though they were very different, the two gardens blended together well: Mrs Paxton's so wild that a family of foxes lived in it undisturbed; Katherine's carefully tended but full of luxuriant shrubs and cascading rockery plants and secret corners and fleshy waterlilies floating on its wide, shallow pond.

Half-standing on the collapsed fence, which had become so much a part of the undergrowth that it looked as though it might actually be sprouting, Katherine ripped the black plastic container off the tree roots. The small tabby cat with the bushy face-fur, who had suddenly appeared beside her, watched closely as she lifted the tree into the waiting hole and held it upright. The roots scrabbled at the earthy sides like thin nervous little fingers looking for something to hold on to.

"Now," said Katherine, "we must take turns to shovel in earth — and think of a memory."

At that moment all the random shouts and bangs from next door stopped. And then the singing started. Just one voice at first, joined almost at once by a lot of others.

"That's jolly!" said Katherine.

"Country and Western," said Flora, making a face.

"Gospel," said Grandma, unexpectedly.

"Whatever it is, it'll be good for the tree," said Katherine. "Plants respond well to music. Come on."

Flora scooped up the first spadeful of earth and threw it on top of the roots. It covered a few, filtered down through the rest and slipped out of sight. An ant struggled free of the avalanche and ran up the flimsy trunk. The cat, caught in a shower of powdery soil, skittered away out of range.

Flora said, "Here's my memory: the way she made it look like fun to use a walking frame, and the way her silver bracelets rattled against it as she went along."

"The way she grew her thumbnail long," said Jack, grabbing the spade from his sister, "to rip open parcels." He held his spadeful of earth as high as he could, as though he was going to do something dramatic with it, and then tipped it and dribbled the earth off gently, sharing it out carefully over the still exposed roots.

He handed the spade to Lisa.

Lisa was quiet for a moment, and then she said, "The way, when she made marmalade or cakes, she always brought us some." She smiled at Jack and dribbled the earth carefully, just as he had. "And the way she used to say she'd knock Mum's block off if Mum tried to give her money for the stuff she'd used."

10

She passed the spade to Grandma.

But Grandma kept her hands at her sides. "Gospel singers," she said softly, and began to hum along with them.

"Grandma has to plant it, too," said Jack. "She was Mrs Paxton's best friend."

"She's here, that's enough," said Katherine, and she took the spade from Lisa. "Mrs Paxton would understand." She scraped the remaining earth into place so that the hole was completely filled. "The way she said she didn't like cats," she said, "but always talked to Tabitha if she thought no one was looking."

"Who *are* those people?" said Flora, looking across at the singing house.

"No idea," said Katherine, pressing the earth down over the roots with one gum-booted foot. "It sounds as if there are dozens of them in there."

"What kind of tree is it?" said Lisa, who hadn't thought to wonder before. She touched one of the little whippety branches gently.

"A hazel," said Katherine. "For Hazel Paxton."

Next door, the singing stopped. A few seconds later all the hammering and movement started up again.

"Neat!" said Jack. "They sang the tree in." He stood on his hands and clapped his feet together.

Just then there was an extra loud thud from next door and a youngish man ran into the garden, bent double, his hand clamped in his armpit. A voice from inside called after him, "Are you all right?"

"Yes," said the man, withdrawing his hand from his armpit rather cautiously, as though he was afraid it might fall off. He caught sight of the small group around the hazel tree.

"Hi," he said, walking over to them. "I'm Ed. I won't offer to shake hands, if you don't mind – I've just managed to drop a cupboard on my fingers."

"Let me have a look," said Katherine, concerned. She

11

stepped towards him onto the only section of the fallen fence which had not yet begun to rot, so that she looked as though she was standing on a small raft in a sea of nettles and brambles.

Ed shook his head. "It's fine," he said. "Really." He was wearing an old grey tracksuit that had obviously been downgraded into working clothes. There were flaking patches of dried white paint on one leg of it, dark smudges on the knees and what looked like splinters of wood caught in the fibres of one sleeve. On him, though, as Flora remarked later, it looked good.

"Hallo, Ed," said Flora, now. "I'm Flora."

She was standing close enough to Lisa to nudge her surreptitiously, but Lisa refused to look at her, afraid that Ed – who was surely aware that he was very attractive – might understand any exchange of glances.

"I'm so sorry," said Katherine, "I have no manners," and she introduced everyone else. "There is also Tabitha," she said, looking around, "but she seems to have disappeared."

"I know what you need for your injury," said Flora to Ed, joining her mother on the fence-raft. "You need Rescue Remedy."

"Oh yes," said Katherine, "have you come across Rescue Remedy?"

Ed shook his head. "No," he said.

"It's a blend of the essential oils of healing flowers," said Katherine. "It has a miraculous effect. We sell it at the Health Shop and people usually come back for more."

"I have heard of it," said Ed. "I meant – no, I'd rather not, thanks."

"I'll get it," said Flora, turning away.

"No!" said Ed, quite sharply, and then, as Flora turned back, startled, he grinned at her and shrugged helplessly "I didn't mean to shout," he said. "I'm just not very comfortable with alternative medicine. By the way, I'm sorry we're

12

making such a noise. We'll have it straight soon, and it'll be quieter."

"That's OK," said Katherine. She and Flora were still looking slightly startled at the vehemence of his reaction to the offered Remedy.

"Only a few of us will be living here, of course," Ed went on, perfectly relaxed and smiling again, seeming to assume they already knew something about the set-up next door. "Not the whole group."

"Group?" said Jack, his attention caught. "You mean, like rock group?"

"Or Gospel Group, perhaps?" said Katherine.

Ed shook his head. "We have our own name for ourselves," he said, "but something tells me you might call us Jesus Freaks."

· CHAPTER THREE ·

FLORA WOULD HAVE said that her household and
Lisa's were as different as chalk and cheese – except
that she could remember some very dry Wensleydale that
had been distinctly chalky, and she was fairly sure you could
have written on a blackboard with the piece of Parmesan
Katherine had once found behind the fridge.

However, there was no doubt that the households were
different.

Not even the decision-making processes were alike. While
Katherine tended to consult the planets, Lisa's parents preferred to turn to *Which*. While Katherine chose colours for
their probable effect on the psyche of those who would live
with them, Lisa's parents had other criteria – that new
things should match existing things, and that all things
should be in shades least likely to show the dirt.

Lisa's house smelt as though someone had recently dem-
onstrated every available paint stripper, tile adhesive, bath
cleaner, furniture polish, carpet shampoo and washing
powder simultaneously; except on Sundays, when it smelt
of roasting meat and stewing apple.

Flora's house smelt of pot-plant compost and candle wax
and toasted cheese and cinnamon; except on Thursdays
when a friend of Katherine's came round to give Grandma
her aromatherapy session, using subtly scented oils which

were not able to rejoin the broken links in her memory, but which were able to stop her fussing about them.

Lisa's home was well-equipped with cupboards whose doors were kept closed on the food, clothes, tools and pre-occupations of the family.

Flora's house was short on cupboards and the doors of those that were there tended to be left open. In Flora's home things were kept on shelves, or piled on chairs, or heaped on the floor, or pinned to huge cork notice-boards.

In Lisa's home you could see the occupants liked calm and order.

In Flora's home you could see they liked candles, news-paper articles on scientific discoveries, cats, astrology, wild-flowers (especially medicinal herbs), birds (especially vul-tures), football, Ancient Egypt, cooking, postcards – and brightly painted wooden birds and animals from Bali, a whole menagerie of which stood about on the floor, except for the flying frog, which hung from the ceiling.

Lisa preferred Flora's house.

As soon as Mrs Paxton's successors were established, Lisa's parents asked around the neighbourhood to see if anyone knew anything about them. No one did.

Katherine, on the other hand, consulted the Ephemeris, the astrologer's timetable, to see where the planets had stood at the time of the meeting with Ed. She would have preferred to look up the moment at which the newcomers had actually taken possession of the house but, not knowing when that was, she decided the instant of first contact would be nearly as good. She considered the small print of the planetary tables for a while and then said that it seemed to her that the heavens had been highlighting communication and revelation.

"That sounds about right," said Flora.

Not surprisingly, the families also reacted differently to the new neighbours, who continued to be quite noisy. Their garden gate clanged regularly as visitors came and went;

cheerful, rhythmic singing beat out morning and evening, even when the windows were closed; and the sudden glad shouts that often followed the songs inspired Lisa's father to rename the house Hallelujah Hall. The car, which Ed explained was a gift from the American founders of the Movement, was also quite a focus of interest in the street, especially when Jesus stickers appeared all around the edges of its windows.

Lisa's father shrugged and made jokes. Her mother, on the other hand, complained that she found it all rather embarrassing. Lisa became aware of this one Saturday when she was sitting on the kitchen table watching her parents redecorate the wall behind the sink. They had covered it with tiles – mostly white though every seventh one had a little blue flower on it – and were busy doing something or other to them, working from opposite ends of the wall towards each other.

All at once her mother stepped back and said, "Oh, this is *too* much."

Lisa thought she meant the tiles.

"It's not too much, they look nice," she said. She didn't really have an opinion about them either way, but the thought of her mother taking them off and starting all over again made her feel tired.

"No, I mean all this wretched chanting," said her mother. "If it's this loud in here, think what it must be like in Katherine's. It never stops."

"It does," said Lisa's father. "It stops for hours. It just goes in bursts – a morning burst and an evening burst, and then at weekends a sort of midday burst."

"Well, they're very long bursts," said her mother, "and it's unsettling. All magical, mystical self-delusion is unsettling. People who get drawn into stuff like that always end up getting obsessive."

"You don't mind Katherine being into astrology," said Lisa.

16

"I don't think she's very serious about that," said her mother. "Anyway, she never talks to me about it."

Lisa was distracted from the subject under discussion by the thought that two years of continuous home improvements might have come to an end.

"Is that the kitchen done, then?" she said, glancing around. "Now the tiles are on? Are we going to start having food that doesn't taste of paint and glue and stuff?"

Her mother laughed, but not as though she thought anything was particularly funny. "Hardly," she said. "The cupboards behind you are a disgrace. And don't sit on that table, you'll weaken it."

Lisa wriggled off the table and stood up, her face flushed. "I'm sorry if I'm too fat for the furniture," she said.

"I didn't say you were fat," said her mother, "I meant tables shouldn't be sat on."

"You're just as obsessed as they are," said Lisa, aggressively. "They're obsessed with Jesus and you're obsessed with fixing the house."

"That's enough," said her father. "Why are you sitting watching us anyway? Why don't you give a hand with the grouting?"

"What's grouting?" said Lisa.

Her father turned slowly to face her, smacking himself lightly on the forehead as he did so. He was laughing, but Lisa, who had seen the gesture many times before, didn't join in. She was sure she knew what he was going to say next: *Trust me to have a daughter who doesn't know what grouting is.*

"Trust me," he said, "to have a daughter who doesn't know what grouting is, even though she's been watching two experts in action for the past half-hour."

"You're always saying I'm fat and stupid," said Lisa, "so why are you surprised?"

"I wish you wouldn't go on about being fat," said her mother. "It's so silly to snipe at me just because I watch

17

your diet. People who are allowed to put on too much weight at your age can spend the rest of their lives trying to lose it."

"So you mean I'm doing a whole lifetime's dieting in one year?" said Lisa. "Isn't that a bit ambitious?"

"There's no point talking to you when you're in this mood," said her mother, "and anyway I can't concentrate with all that holy intoning going on."

Next door, one house closer to the worshippers, Katherine was rattled too, but for quite a different reason. She was struck with sadness that Ed had been so sure of meeting prejudice that he had used the phrase 'Jesus Freaks' himself, rather than have it thrown at him. She listened to the voices, and then to the silence that followed the voices, and tried to remember what she had said to him, out in the garden the first time they'd met. She couldn't be sure that she'd made it clear enough that religious persecution was not one of her sins.

She decided she would say something reassuring to him, or to one of the others, next time she encountered them, either in the garden or in town. Several of them, it had turned out, worked locally – Ed at the bank next to Katherine's Health Shop and others in the Post Office, the dry cleaners, the library.

Jack, equally unaffected by the new arrivals and by the anxieties of the established residents, simply continued with the latest stage of his Vulture Appreciation Project. He was attempting to make a vulture mobile, to hang in front of the vulture posters and above the vulture models (which were stuck onto model carcasses). He was hardly aware that he was jigging to the beat of the Gospel songs as he worked.

Flora, though, admitted to Lisa on the quiet that she did find herself thinking about Ed from time to time. "I know it's unrealistic," she said wistfully. "He's into a whole different world view."

"He's too old for you, anyway," said Lisa.

"No one's too old to *fantasise* about," said Flora. "I can fantasise about King Arthur, if I want to, or Merlin. But I do need to believe we'd have *something* in common."

"He invited you in," said Lisa, "just after he said they were Jesus Freaks. I was there, I heard him."

"Only to make up for snapping at me about Rescue Remedy," said Flora. "Anyway, what he actually said was 'Our House Services are open to all – come and find out more about us.' It wasn't personal."

"You could still go," said Lisa.

"They don't play my kind of music," said Flora. Then she winked at Lisa. "You go!" she said, not really meaning it. "You go, and tell me about it."

"Mum'd freak out if I went in there," said Lisa.

"Would you like to?" said Flora, her attention caught. "Are you interested?"

"No," said Lisa, truthfully.

"What *is* your stand, then?" said Flora. "My mum's all for spiritual freedom, your mum is embarrassed, your dad thinks it's a laugh. What do *you* think?"

"It's not so much that I think it's a laugh," said Lisa, "I just can't understand how people can dedicate their whole lives to just one thing."

"I can," said Flora. "I think it would be great. Imagine if you found something you really believed in and sang its praises all day! That's probably what we're all meant to do, if we only knew it."

"Dad says it's a waste of energy," said Lisa. "It's all a delusion, they're singing their heads off and no one's hearing them but us."

"I think they're heard," said Flora. "I think if you really believe, and you do what your belief tells you, you are heard."

"Who by?" said Lisa.

"Him, her, it," said Flora. "I don't know if it matters what you call it, I don't expect anyone knows its real name.

19

Mum calls it 'The Creative Principle of the Universe' – but that's a shade long for everyday use."

"Dad says the universe is one big accident," said Lisa.

"Do you know how much you quote him?" said Flora, suddenly irritated. "They're not necessarily right about everything, you know."

"It makes sense to me," said Lisa.

"Yes, but does it?" said Flora. "Or is it that you're too lazy to think about it?"

"It isn't obligatory to disagree with your parents," said Lisa, who was also beginning to feel irritated. "You agree with Katherine most of the time."

"It's fine to agree if you really *do*," said Flora. "But it's feeble just to accept things."

"I don't want to fight with you over people we don't even know," said Lisa.

"I'm not fighting," said Flora. She took off her bracelet and shook it in Lisa's ear so that all its tiny silver moons and stars chinked together with a sound like distant bells. "I'm trying to wake you up!"

Lisa laughed. "I am awake," she said, pushing her eyelids up with her thumbs to demonstrate. "Let's forget it. Let's just ignore them, OK?"

Some things, however, don't choose to be ignored. Early one evening the neighbours, having got the house the way they wanted it, emerged in pairs, and began to ring door-bells all along the street.

· CHAPTER FOUR ·

W HEN THE BROKEN bell on Katherine's front door
let out the best electrical croak it could manage, an
answering squawk came from Jack's room, above the porch.
"Aaaargh, don't open it!" he shouted. "It's the Hallelujah
lot, come to get us."

In the room across the landing, Flora looked at Lisa, over
a pile of homework books, and began to giggle. Then
Katherine was running up the stairs, two at a time, her long
cotton skirt catching on the treads.

"Be quiet, Jack, they'll hear you!" she hissed, glaring in
through his bedroom door. "It isn't kind and it isn't polite
to jeer at people, and please don't do it."

"OK," said Jack, startled.

"And get back into bed," said Katherine. "You're supposed to be going to sleep, not watching out of the
window."

"Mum's feeling guilty," Flora whispered to Lisa, as
Katherine ran downstairs again. "That's why she's ratty."

"Why guilty?" said Lisa. "What are you on about?"

"I bet she agrees with Jack, secretly," said Flora, going
onto the landing and hanging over the bannister rail to
watch as Katherine strode to the door, skirt swirling and
bangles knocking importantly on her arms. "She knows
when she opens up there'll be strangers on the step with
leaflets, wanting to talk about God. And that's not how she

likes to spend her evenings. Come on, let's get a look at them."

In fact, although there were two people on the step, only one was a stranger, a smiling middle-aged woman with bouncy, glossy hair. With her was Ed. Flora had been right about the leaflets, though.

"Hallo again," said Ed, with his engaging grin, and did the introductions. The woman, whose name was Barbara Marsh, was dressed casually in a tracksuit top and a skirt. Ed was in jeans and a white sweatshirt. Across the chest of the sweatshirt there were two lines of black lettering which read, ALL FOR THE LOVE OF JESUS. He looked past Katherine to Lisa and Flora and pointed to his chest. "All kitted out now, you see," he said. "What do you think?"

"It certainly makes a statement!" said Flora.

It was the only statement of its kind, as it turned out, that either of them did make that evening.

They wouldn't come in but stood leaning on the slender porch pillars, relaxed and informal, and apologised again for the noise they had made doing up the house. In fact, they did more, they apologised for not apologising sooner, and that set Katherine off into a stream of apologies for not having called to welcome them to their new home.

"We only heard the hammering and stuff when we were in the garden," said Flora, deciding they'd got stuck in a loop-tape of apologies and needed to be got out of it. "The singing gets everywhere, though."

Barbara Marsh smiled at her. "I hope it doesn't upset you?" she said.

"It's fine," said Katherine hastily, "but maybe I should warn you there was a bit of a drama last year about some people in the block of flats down by the church. They had their stereo on full blast all summer, with the windows open, and there were a lot of complaints."

"Heavy Metal doesn't appeal to everyone," said Flora.

Barbara Marsh winced.

22

"Well, quite," said Katherine. "That's exactly how I felt. It finally stopped because someone threatened legal action and put the fear of God into them."

Flora snorted and Katherine clamped her hands over her mouth. "Sorry," she mumbled through them. "Figure of speech! I didn't mean to be offensive."

Ed laughed, and Barbara Marsh reached out and touched the back of Katherine's hand lightly. "Don't panic," she said. "We're not from another planet, you know."

"And I don't mean to suggest anyone's likely to set the law on you," said Katherine. "I just thought I should mention that one or two people around here have developed a bit of an allergy to music."

"Mother's getting flustered," said Flora. She put her arm round Katherine's waist and Katherine put her arm round Flora's shoulders. "Relax, Ma," said Flora, "they've told us they're not aliens."

Next to them, Lisa suddenly felt out of it, and lumpish. Katherine and Flora were flowing together inside the door, in a pattern of soft fabrics and unusual jewellery, and Ed and Barbara Marsh were paired outside the door, looking neat and athletic. Lisa stood alone, dressed in no particular style, and contributing nothing.

"I won't keep you," said Barbara Marsh. "In any case we need to move on. We want to knock on as many doors as possible this evening." She held out a leaflet. "Could I ask you to read this?" she said.

Katherine took it. "Of course," she said. Then she glanced down at it and looked back at the two on the doorstep in some surprise. "Drugs!" she said.

"There's quite a flourishing trade around here," said Ed.

"It's important to try to alert everyone," said Barbara, "especially anyone responsible for children or young people."

"Of course," said Katherine again, still looking a bit surprised. "I'd expected something different – I didn't realise

– I mean, I hadn't understood that this was one of your areas of concern."

"What happens to the body affects the spirit," said Barbara, reasonably.

"You could say," said Ed, "that dependence on drugs is a kind of possession. The body is taken over and behaviour is changed. Not for the better, either."

"Don't worry," said Flora lightly. "The most powerful drug we have in this house is aspirin."

"Hey," said Ed, pushing away from the porch pillar with his shoulder so he stood upright, "we're not suggesting . . ."

"No problem," said Katherine. "We're not paranoid, we didn't think we stood accused!"

"We just want to ask everyone to be vigilant," said Barbara. "If people don't realise there's a problem, then they don't notice things – pushers, for example, who are sometimes only teenagers themselves, hanging around schools."

Lisa, feeling she could contribute here, nodded and opened her mouth, but Flora spoke first. "We've had them at our place," she said.

"What!" said Katherine, holding Flora away from her and staring at her. "You never told me."

"They were spotted," said Lisa, suddenly so determined to join in that she spoke rather too loudly. "The police came."

"And were they caught?" said Barbara, sadly, as if she knew the answer.

"No," said Flora, "they ran." She made a face. "They ran before the cop car got there," she said, "so it was no fun, there wasn't even much of a chase. Mr Gurney had a go, but he's not built for speed."

"A couple of the teachers always stand at the gates now, when we go out," said Lisa.

"Unfortunately," said Ed, who wasn't smiling now, "not all schools are so sensible."

"We've set ourselves a programme," said Barbara. "We

24

want to approach every household in town with this warning."

"We patrol the schools, too," said Ed, "as often as we can. We like to think we look a bit less obvious than the average plain-clothes police officer."

"You're not exactly inconspicuous in that sweatshirt," said Flora.

"Flora!" Katherine began, but Ed cut in, "Flora's right," he said. "At times like that I wear a shirt that has nothing to say for itself. We've already made one citizen's arrest."

"I'm impressed," said Katherine.

"Community service," said Ed, turning to go. "The singing's the fun bit."

As Katherine shut the front door on the retreating figures, Flora said, "Mum, you were awful, you gushed!"

"Did I?" said Katherine. "I had my response all ready and then they didn't say what I expected and I was thrown."

Lisa said, "I bet my parents won't speak to them."

"What will they do?" said Flora with interest. "Tell them to push off?"

"No," said Lisa, "they just won't open the door."

A brief surveillance from behind the luxuriant pot plants that screened Katherine's front window proved her right.

"I think I'll go and reassure them," said Katherine. She went out into the dark garden and called across the carefully maintained fence on that side until Lisa's mother opened her kitchen door, spilling light all over her trim lawn. "Valerie, it's all right," she said, as Lisa's mother came over to the fence, Goldie staggering at her heels. "They're OK. They didn't come to preach at all."

"I'm afraid we hid," said Valerie. "I can cope with strangers yattering about salvation on the doorstep, but you feel you can't be rude when it's neighbours, don't you? But then I didn't want to encourage them, either."

Goldie sat down and gave a huge, creaking yawn.

"It wasn't like that," said Katherine, "honestly."

25

"They were just ordinary," Lisa shrugged.

"Keep your voice down," said her mother. "They can't be far down the road, they'll hear you."

"It's OK, they won't put a hex on us," said Flora.

"That's a relief," said Valerie. "I must say, I keep wishing they hadn't bought the wretched house. What on earth did they want to move in here for, anyway?"

"They may be noisy," said Flora, "but they're not weird."

"When you come to think of it," said Katherine, "we're the ones who are weird. I mean, this *is* supposed to be a Christian country and here are we, twitching away like anything because we've suddenly got some real Christians living next door!"

The smile faded from Valerie's face. "I go to church," she said, "sometimes."

"You know what I mean," said Katherine. "You're not so up-front about it."

"You don't have the T-shirt!" said Flora.

"You don't have the music!" said Lisa.

"Listen to this," said Katherine, holding the leaflet in the beam of light coming from the kitchen door, and reading the drugs warning aloud.

"Good guys, see?" said Flora.

"It certainly seems so," said Valerie.

"It says here," said Katherine, "that they're also campaigning to get a video shop behind the station closed down. Apparently they've been allowing quite young children to hire some really revolting stuff, all to do with Satanism and black magic. Yup, they're good guys, and we'll just have to get rid of our prejudices."

"I'll try," said Valerie. "And in the meantime, do you want to get rid of my daughter? It's time she was going to bed."

"I'll get my stuff," said Lisa.

"Lisa," said Katherine, "do you mind going home by the front way and dropping something in at Hallelujah Hall as

26

you go? I just want to write a very quick note – I'm going to volunteer for drug patrol."

"Oh, Mum!" said Flora. "You were *nice* to them, they don't know you misjudged them. You don't have to go *that* far."

"Anyway, you're at the shop when school comes out," said Lisa.

"I can be flexible," said Katherine. "I can take a late lunch-break. It's important. I'd like to help."

"Careful," said Valerie, only half-joking, "they'll convert you."

"Maybe they will," said Katherine, cheerfully. "And maybe I'd like it. Whatever they've got, it certainly makes them happy."

As Lisa turned in at the front gate of Mrs Paxton's old house, she saw that all the front windows were dark. It seemed that no one was at home. As she neared the front door, though, she began to hear something. Deep inside the house someone was crying, great choking sobs which turned into gulping coughs and then faded into the sort of forlorn weeping that sounded as though it could go on for a very long time.

Lisa shivered, slipped the piece of paper through the letter-box, and ran home.

· CHAPTER FIVE ·

I F THE ENERGIES were green on the day the tree was
planted, then they were certainly red on the night the
man ran screaming down Cemetery Road.

Jack saw the first signs. It was after ten o'clock, but he
had grown steadily livelier all evening – mainly, so Katherine said, because the moon was passing through Scorpio.
Neither bribes nor threats could persuade him up to his
room until well after his usual time. Even then, he didn't
get into bed, but climbed onto a chair to unhook the vul-
ture-mobile from the centre light. He wanted to attach it,
instead, to the curtain rail, so that it would hang in front
of the window.

While he was struggling with it, he saw three cars glide
quietly along the road, through the opening in the fence,
and on past the allotments.

Even though he raised the bottom sash and stuck his head
out as far as he dared, the stealthy procession moved out
of sight, hidden by the dark bulk of the house next door.

Jack bustled across the landing to Flora's room.

"There are unmarked police cars going up to the railway
hut," he said. "Quick, let's see out of your window."

"How do you know they're police cars," said Flora, pulling her curtains back, "if they're not marked."

"I just do," said Jack.

"Nothing's happened out there for months," said Flora.

28

"Open the window," said Jack, "so we can hear."

"Hear what!" said Flora, but she did open it, and they leant on the sill, side by side, waiting for their eyes to grow accustomed to the darkness.

The moon, which was almost full, was large and low in the sky, but it was a curious rusty colour, all its wide craters and low mountain ridges clearly visible. It seemed to reflect no light at all. At the edge of the allotments the remains of a bonfire glowed and died by turns, sometimes invisible, sometimes brighter than the huge globe of rock that floated above it. Way beyond, in the direction of the railway line, there was a curious pattern of pale orange streaks, so narrow and so faint that it was necessary to look to one side of them in order to see them at all.

Jack nudged Flora and pointed, and Flora nodded. They both knew what it was – the light of a lamp leaking out through the cracks and splits in the ancient hut, with its arcane graffiti of nicknames and symbols, and the broken padlock hanging from its door.

They stared until they felt as though their eyes were being pulled out on strings. Gradually, shapes began to make sense, and movement helped, and they understood that they were seeing three cars, with no lights, turning left around the top of the allotments and drifting towards the hut. The shapes of stationary vehicles loomed behind it, and the streaks of light that criss-crossed it dimmed and flickered as figures moved inside.

Apart from the angry stare of the red moon, it was a peaceful scene, silent and dreamlike, and when it broke into violent action Flora was so startled that she jumped and banged her head on the bottom of the open window.

She and Jack sensed rather than saw the hut door fly open. They half-saw and half-heard the scuffles that broke out, among how many figures they couldn't judge. They clutched each other as the car headlights flared, the car doors creaked and slammed, and all became distant, blurry confusion.

But the thing that was clear, the thing that made them almost stop breathing – safe and out of it though they were – was the figure that separated itself from the rest and came capering down the road, past the allotments, towards the fence opening. It was a thin and spiky figure, moving oddly, jerkily, and the flat reddish light from the huge, dead, unreal-looking moon gave it the colour of dried blood. As it ran its crooked run, it screamed, a weird thin high wailing scream, that might have had words in it and might not.

"It's a demon," whispered Jack, and he clung to Flora as he hadn't done since he was three years old.

"Why don't they chase it?" hissed Flora, hugging Jack almost as much to comfort herself as him. "Why don't they stop it!"

"Quick!" said Jack, pulling free, and he shot back across the landing to his own window, with Flora so close behind him that the toes of her shoes kicked the heels of his.

By the time they were looking out of Jack's window, with its view of the road, the figure was already through the fence opening. It had stopped its horrible, wild, jerky run but it was still moving fast, and it was still letting out its harsh, high-pitched screaming chant, which was now so loud that windows and doors were opening all along the street.

"It's going to Hallelujah Hall!" said Jack softly, whispering even though it couldn't possibly have heard him above the uproar it was making.

"One of the police cars is coming," said Flora. The car was not in sight from that angle, but the beam of its approaching headlights was highlighting the fading allotment bonfire. "Come on, let's go down."

Katherine was already on the porch, Lisa and her parents were at their open front door, heads were silhouetted in the

30

windows of the flats opposite, and even in the windows of the big block right down by the church.

Standing beside Katherine, Flora and Jack had a clearer view of the screaming man. From closer-to he looked human, but certainly not normal, as he beat with his fists on the door of Mrs Paxton's old house.

Even though they could hear what he was saying, they still didn't understand. He was cursing someone, damning someone, wishing every plague and misery known to heaven or to hell upon someone. Then he stopped pounding the door and began dragging something to and fro along his arm, something that glittered in the moonlight, something that seemed to leave dark marks on his skin as it passed across it.

"Oh no!" said Katherine. "He's cutting himself," and she began to run down the path. Before she had gone far, though, the door opened and Ed and another man appeared, and then they were holding the screaming man by the arms, and Barbara Marsh was there too, talking to him, calmly but loudly, above his noise.

"She didn't betray you," Barbara Marsh was saying. "She didn't tell the police anything, they must have found out some other way."

Katherine hesitated near the gate, and then walked slowly back up the path, unable to prevent herself from staring. Flora and Jack joined her, silent and wide-eyed.

"You've turned her mind," the man was shouting, his voice now hoarse with overuse. "You've brain-washed her, bring her out here, make her face what she did . . . they're crawling up my arms, they're underneath my skin, they're swimming in my veins, get them out, get them out, get them out!"

The doors of the police car opened before it stopped, and two police officers threw themselves out of it and ran up the path.

Seeing them, the man went limp and sagged at the knees

31

so that Ed and the other man, who had been holding him back, were now holding him up.

Barbara Marsh stepped round in front of them and said to the first police officer, in her clear calm voice, "I'm afraid he needs an ambulance."

Although Lisa's parents were not in the habit of staring at fights or accidents, the scene on the doorstep of Hallelujah Hall was so extreme, so bizarre, that it seemed pointless to pretend not to be watching. They walked over to stand beside Katherine, and Lisa joined Flora and Jack, each of them as white-faced as the others.

While one police officer radioed for an ambulance, the other asked Barbara if anyone needed emergency first aid. "There seems to be rather a lot of blood," he said, looking at the stains on Ed's sweatshirt.

"It's all from this poor soul," said Barbara, resting her hand briefly on the bowed head of the young man, who hung between his two supporters almost like a figure plucked from a crucifix. "And all the wounds are self-inflicted, but fortunately not deep."

She stooped and picked up something from between his feet, then held it out. "Broken glass," she said. "I imagine you interrupted the assignation out there before he'd had his fix – he seems to be suffering acute withdrawal symptoms."

"We'll take him from you, sir," said the policewoman to Ed, but Ed said, "It's OK, let's wait for the ambulance. He's relaxed at the moment – we don't want to risk setting him off again."

Although the ambulance was extraordinarily quick, the man was unconscious by the time it arrived. Barbara followed the stretcher down the path and then, just as the ambulance crew was hitching it up to lift it inside, she bent and kissed the forehead of the figure that lay, unmoving now, under a red blanket, and said, "Jesus will heal you. Trust in Him."

Then she did something completely unexpected. She

turned and walked straight up to the little group huddled in the middle of Katherine's path. Later they all agreed that, for one moment, they had thought she was going to accuse them of being unfeelingly curious. Far from it, though. She had come to apologise for all the upset.

"He seemed completely out of his mind," said Katherine.

"Totally possessed by the drug," said Barbara. "His girl-friend has taken refuge with us and he's been trying to get her back. She's been very strong-minded and refused, and in his muddled state he seems to have decided she set the police on him, which she didn't. And neither, as it happens, did we — though only because we didn't have the infor-mation."

"And is she all right?" said Katherine. "The girlfriend?"

"Thank the Lord she wasn't chemically addicted," said Barbara. "We caught her in time. She was very bound up in the life-style, though, and it isn't easy for her to break out of that. Especially as her boyfriend and some of the others have been putting a lot of pressure on her."

"I think I may have heard her crying," said Lisa.

"I expect you have," said Barbara. "It's the thing she does most, just at the moment. But the longer she stays with us, the higher our chances of helping her to get free of it all."

"Has she no parents?" said Lisa's father.

"She was brought up in care," said Barbara, "and when we found her, she was sleeping rough."

"I think I saw her," said Jack, "looking out of the window while the man was screaming." He pointed. "That window," he said, "above your front door. Is that where you keep her?"

"It's her room," said Barbara, "but we don't 'keep' her — she stays because she chooses to, she's not a prisoner." Suddenly her eyes filled with tears. "Though I'd be very tempted to imprison someone," she said, "if it was the only way to save them from becoming like . . ." She stopped, sniffed, and said, "Sorry – but when I think of that young life, thrown away . . ."

"Can we help at all?" said Katherine. "Would she like to come in for a meal sometime, for a change of scene . . . ? I did volunteer to help with the school patrols, but I'd be happy to do anything . . ."

"She'll be fine," said Barbara. "And thank you for your note. I've been meaning to talk to you about that. I'll get back to you sometime." She glanced over her shoulder.

While they had all been talking, the two police officers had finished taking statements from Ed and his companion and had driven off, and the cars that had been up by the railway hut had begun to make their way out through the fence gap again, travelling faster this time, and with more people on board.

Now, as Barbara turned, the last of them whisked past the gate, portable blue light clamped to the roof and flashing, but siren silent. "Everything's all right now," she said, and turned back, smiling. "All calm and peaceful."

Flora nudged Lisa and pointed upwards. The moon was no longer low and red and watchful. As it had risen in the night sky, so it seemed to have withdrawn from the earth, and now it sailed high – cool and white and carefree.

· CHAPTER SIX ·

ABOUT THREE DAYS later, Jack came leaping down the stairs to Saturday breakfast, burbling with excitement about what he'd seen from the bathroom window. "They're hacking through the jungle with machetes," he said, making swiping movements with his right arm, "and I'm going in to ask if I can have some feathers."

Grandma smiled at him and shook the cereal packet invitingly.

Katherine said to Flora, "Have you any idea what he's talking about?"

"No," said Flora, going to the window, "but there *is* a lot of crashing and crunching going on in Mrs Paxton's garden. Any connection, Jack?"

"There'll be all sorts under there," said Jack, making straight for the kitchen door. As he opened it, he was faced with Lisa and her mother approaching through the garden.

"I'm making a vulture mask for the Hallowe'en party," he said to them by way of greeting. "I need some big real feathers."

"Can't help you there, Jack," said Lisa, but he was too busy wriggling past them to hear.

Lisa went on into the kitchen, but her mother stood where she was, just outside the door.

"Come in, Valerie," Katherine called, assuming that Lisa's mother, who kept to an unspoken rule about short-

35

cuts through the garden, was waiting for an invitation. The rule seemed perfectly simple to Valerie. It was acceptable, she felt, for either household to step over the fence and visit the other via the back door so long as they were expected. If they were not expected, it was proper to go to the front door and ring the bell. Katherine, who operated very few rules, had never entirely grasped this. She just knew that Valerie could be a bit formal sometimes.

In fact, Valerie was expected today – she was giving Katherine a lift to the supermarket – and the only reason she was standing outside the door was because she was temporarily fascinated by all the seething activity in the garden on the other side. Not machetes, perhaps, but scythes certainly, were sweeping through the tangled weeds as eight or nine people attacked the overgrown undergrowth with cheerful vigour.

"Come out and look at this," Valerie called in through the door.

The chilly air, which overnight had stopped feeling as though it belonged to autumn and had begun to suggest early winter instead, was heavy with the green smell of slashed vegetation.

"I suppose it should have been obvious they'd start on the garden," said Katherine rather wistfully, "once they'd finished the house."

Jack, hurrying in amongst all the industry, had no problems about crossing fences. He had been so young when the one on that side had fallen down that he had no memory of it ever standing, and no real sense that the two gardens represented separate territories.

"Jack, watch out!" yelled Flora, suddenly very conscious of the sharp blades swinging.

But the scythers were aware of Jack's approach and those nearest him stopped well before he was within range.

"Yes," said Barbara Marsh, who was holding a heavy-looking pair of shears, with sap-stains on the blades, "of course you can look around for dropped feathers. But a vulture mask doesn't sound very nice – can't you think of something more attractive to make?"

"People aren't fair to vultures," said Jack. "I like them."

"They don't have very nice habits," said Barbara, smiling down at him.

"They eat dead bodies," said Jack. "If they didn't eat them they'd just rot and stink . . ."

"Yes," said Barbara, interrupting him briskly, "but I don't think it's something we need to dwell on."

Ed strolled over, holding out a glossy blue-black feather. "Part of a magpie's tail any good to you?" he said.

Katherine, watching from a distance, said, "He was right, there are feathers over there."

"He'll have been thinking of the foxes. The foxes will have killed birds and taken them to their den," said Flora.

"Oh, the foxes!" said Katherine. "I was forgetting. A lot of wildlife must have got established in there over the years."

"They're finding him more feathers," said Lisa, "look."

"I wonder," said Katherine, half to herself, "if I could possibly ask them to leave just *some* bits of it wild . . . I know it's their garden and all that, but it does seem a shame . . ."

"It *is* their garden," said Valerie, "and it's high time it was tamed. The seeds from some of those weeds used to come over as far as us – you must get them here, too, surely?"

"Up to a point," said Katherine. "This garden is so full of stuff there's not much space for anything else to get a hold . . . but if you *will* have neat little beds, with gaps between the plants . . ."

"I hope they're not scything the foxes," said Flora.

"The foxes will have gone at the first sign of disturbance," said Katherine. "I suppose it's all right, really; it's the proper time of year for the young ones to be leaving home anyway."

"If they head for bandit-country," said Flora, "they'll have a problem. There are three others living there that *I* know about, and there are probably more."

"There are other places, I suppose," said Katherine, "but I can't help feeling a bit sad about it – there's some distinction in having a fox family for neighbours."

"I was never keen on them," said Valerie.

"They didn't come in our garden," said Lisa.

"We may not have seen them," said her mother, "but I smelt them sometimes. And if you go out early you can often smell if they've passed down the street. You must have noticed it, Katherine, it's quite strong."

"You worry too much about smells," said Katherine. "*Life* smells."

"It doesn't have to," said Valerie firmly. "Not these days."

Jack leapt onto the collapsed fence and stood in triumph, holding up a fistful of assorted feathers. "Look what I've got from Hallelujah Hall!" he shouted across to them. The second the words were spoken he realised what he'd said, and turned to look back at the working party in horror, as if he didn't know whether to apologise or run.

Barbara Marsh walked over to him, and she was laughing.

"It's quite all right," she said, loud enough for the group by Katherine's door to hear as well. "We heard a rumour about our nickname – we *love* it!"

"It wasn't meant to be offensive," called Katherine, who didn't really know how Lisa's father had meant it.

"Well, of course not," said Barbara. "How could it be offensive? Do you know what Hallelujah means, Jack?"

"It's what you shout," said Jack, nervously, "after the singing."

"It means Praise God," said Barbara. "What could be nicer than to be known as 'Praise God Hall'!"

Jack escaped with all possible speed and took himself and his feathers off to his room.

Katherine and Valerie went shopping.

Flora and Lisa got irritated with each other across the remains of the breakfast on the table, trying all the while to keep smiling so that Grandma, who was working her way through the contents of the refilled teapot, wouldn't be upset.

"We don't want to be here for Jack's Hallowe'en party, do we?" said Flora.

Lisa shrugged. "I thought we were supposed to help," she said.

"We can help decorate the house," said Flora, "but we don't necessarily have to stay and be over-run by lots of junior ghouls and ghosts."

"Where'd we go?" said Lisa.

"Mel's having a party," said Flora, ticking names off on her fingers, "and so is Carole . . . and . . . oh, maybe that's all."

"I'm not invited to those," said Lisa.

"You are!" said Flora. "The whole class is. We can choose, or we can go to one and then the other."

"I am *not* invited," said Lisa crossly. "I'm fat and boring and they don't want me."

"How often do I have to tell you?" said Flora. "You are *not fat!*"

"Ok," said Lisa, and then, realising that she was beginning to shout, she flashed an extra-wide smile at Grandma, who smiled back. "But would your clothes fit me? Would they? *Would they?*"

"No," said Flora, "because we're different physical types. But just because we're not the *same* shape doesn't mean that either of us is the *wrong* shape." She glared at Lisa briefly, beamed at Grandma, and said, "And if some of them think you're boring it's only because you never open your mouth when there's more than three people in a room."

"That's because I don't like it when there's more than three people in a room," said Lisa.

Suddenly, Flora giggled. "Let's go somewhere else," she said. "I'm beginning to feel I belong in Hallelujah Hall."

"How do you mean?" said Lisa.

"All this smiling," said Flora. "Haven't you noticed how they all smile all the time?"

"It is hard," said Lisa, with a quick protective glance at Grandma, who had invited Tabitha onto her lap and was dreamily stroking the small glossy head, "to argue with someone when you've both got grins plastered on your faces."

"Maybe that's why they do it," said Flora, thoughtfully.

"Do you mean they keep smiling so they can't argue?" said Lisa. "Or do you mean they keep smiling to hide the fact that they're longing to have a right good go at each other?"

"Interesting question," said Flora. "I'd love to know the answer."

"Listen to them," said Lisa, suddenly aware of the steady background sound of chopping and hacking that was floating in from next door. "I bet they'll have it all clear by lunch-time."

In fact, it took them until tea-time, and it was only when every weed had fallen, the workers had gone indoors, and the singing was well under way, that Katherine noticed something slightly odd. She led Flora out into the fading light to show it to her, too.

"See," she said. "They've cleared away the fallen fence – another old friend gone – and they're obviously going to put up a new one." She pointed. "There's the little trench they've made, to mark where it's going to be."

"Doesn't it look empty," said Flora, staring in amazement

at the green desert that had replaced the familiar jungle. The trees around the edges had not been touched, but the tangled brambles and bristly thistles, the ragged robin with its hairy white seeds, the pink, blue and white Michaelmas daisies, the straggling columbine, the jaunty ragwort, the stinging nettles, and even the conventional garden plants that had fought for a living among it all, had been cut to the ground and piled into three enormous heaps.

"But look where the trench *is*," said Katherine. "You haven't realised what they've done because it all looks so different. Listen, the old fence fell over towards us, right? And they've marked the line for the new one where the top of it was lying, instead of where the bottom of it was."

Flora stared.

"I'm sure it's a genuine mistake," said Katherine, "but if they put the new fence up where they plan to, they'll be pinching a strip about three feet wide from our garden!"

· CHAPTER SEVEN ·

"YOU *MUST SPEAK* to them about it!" said Lisa's mother, sitting at Katherine's kitchen table and surreptitiously wiping the rim of her coffee mug with her thumb before drinking out of it. She wore the same sort of neat blouse and skirt on a Sunday as she did on weekdays when, as Katherine said, she at least had the excuse that she was behind the counter at the Gas Showroom.

Yet — even though Valerie had once asked Katherine if the wooden animals were hard to dust, a question Katherine couldn't answer because it had never occurred to her to try; and even though Lisa's father Harry had once offered to help Katherine redecorate, so soon after she had done it herself that it was almost insulting — the two families got on surprisingly well, and usually spent some time together on a Sunday. If it happened in Lisa's house, both Jack and Flora found they had other things to do. If it was at Flora's house, though, Lisa always came along.

Today the two girls, at the opposite end of the big table from the three adults, were sniggering together over the Sunday papers and Jack was in the sitting room, watching a video.

"I suppose I should say something," said Katherine reluctantly.

"Of course you should," said Harry, helping himself to a ginger biscuit.

"Mum, you *have* to," said Flora, temporarily abandoning a story about the hyperactive love-life of a new group whose extraordinary revelations just happened to coincide with the release of their new album. "We can't let them steal half our garden."

"Hardly half!" said Katherine. "It's a very narrow strip. Anyway, I think they're out today, it's very quiet in there. I suppose they're at church."

"I'll tell you something, though," said Valerie. "They don't go to St Mary's. I've just come back from morning service and none of them were there."

"You've been to church!" said Katherine. "It isn't Christmas!"

"Mum!" said Flora reprovingly, but Valerie only laughed. "I realised I'd been a bit prejudiced about them," she said, "so I thought I'd be polite and join them down the road. It's only for an hour, after all."

"Hey," Flora hissed at Lisa, holding up her paper to give them both a screen of newsprint, "you didn't tell me! Were you hoping to make a good impression on Ed?"

"I didn't go," Lisa hissed back. "I had homework." She pushed the paper aside and reached out for a biscuit; then saw her mother's frown, and withdrew her hand without taking one.

"And I didn't go," said Harry, who had heard the whispered exchange, "because more people have murdered and tortured and burned each other in the name of organised religion than for any other single reason, and I am not in favour of encouraging it."

"So there!" said Lisa.

"Can't argue with that!" said Flora.

"You look amazingly cheerful," said Katherine, "for someone who's just written off a significant chunk of human experience."

"Only because I'm not thinking about it," said Harry. "If

43

I thought how many deluded folk there are on this earth, I'd weep."

"Oh well," said Valerie quickly, "Sunday morning church is just a social thing, really. It was a shame the people I went to socialise with didn't turn up, but still the flowers looked very pretty, and I like Mr Foster; he never asks why I don't go more often."

"True. He never asks me why I don't go at all," said Katherine.

"Aren't you a bit of a pagan to be on chatting terms with a Reverend?" said Valerie.

"I see him sometimes at PTA meetings," said Katherine. "He's got a granddaughter in the junior class."

"Let's get back to this fence business," said Harry. "Would you like me to come with you when you go to complain? Ride shot-gun, as it were."

"No, it's OK thanks," said Katherine.

"But we *are* going to stand up for our territorial rights, aren't we?" said Flora.

Katherine spun the bracelets on her arm, and watched as they revolved their way from her elbow down to her wrist and came to rest there, ringing slightly against each other. Then she made a face. "I'll tell you what's holding me back," she said. "If they continue with the line they're marking out, and set up the new fence along it, Mrs Paxton's memorial tree will end up in Mrs Paxton's old garden . . . I almost wonder if it's meant! Does that sound silly?"

"Yes," said everyone in the room at the same time, and Flora flapped the paper for emphasis until the flying frog revolved on his string.

"And another thing," said Harry, "I grant you they're genuinely well-meaning – right attitude to drugs and all the rest – but they *are* pushy and you want to watch them."

"Oh yes, I forgot," said Valerie. She leant forward across

44

the table, as if she was including everyone in a conspiracy. "They've had a row with the pub!" she said.

"The pub!" said Katherine. "Are they against alcohol, then?"

"Alcohol didn't seem to be the problem," said Harry. "Their big thing is that they want to exorcise the upstairs landing!"

"Great!" said Flora. "Can we watch?"

"It isn't going to happen," said Valerie. "They've been formally banned."

"I should fetch Jack," said Flora, glancing round at the door but not getting up. "He always misses the best gossip."

"I didn't even know the pub *had* a ghost," said Katherine.

"It hasn't," said Harry, "it has a gimmick."

"Flora says it has a ghost," said Lisa.

"Absolutely!" said Flora. "A woman who walks through closed doors!"

"That's what's written on the publicity leaflet," said Harry. "You must learn not to confuse publicity with truth. You can read about Grisly Gloria the Ghostly Gate-crasher, but you don't need to believe in her."

"Is that really what it says on the leaflet?" said Katherine.

"More or less."

"No, it isn't, of course it isn't," said Valerie. "It just says that a few people have seen this woman and thought she was real until she suddenly disappeared. I suppose it *is* a bit of a gimmick, really."

"It'd be good publicity to have it exorcised, wouldn't it?" said Flora. "I bet the press'd come. And local TV, maybe. It'd be great for business!"

"In the short-term, perhaps," said Harry. "But then what? No, these people have to be told they can't meddle with tradition."

"Wait a minute," said Flora, narrowing her eyes. "You say there never was a ghost anyway – so why does it matter if they do an exorcism there? If there never was a ghost in the first place, then nothing'll change, will it?"

"Yes it will, young Flora! If word gets out that the place has been exorcised, then good old landlord Tom can't go on advertising it as haunted, can he? He'll have lost credibility."

"Ah," said Flora. "You're right."

"I've just thought of something," said Katherine. "Why hasn't Mr Foster done something about it, in all these years? The church and the pub are only about a hundred yards apart."

"Yesterday I couldn't have answered that," said Valerie. "But I just found out this morning. You know how vicars hang about at the door when you leave at the end of the service? Oh no, you wouldn't. Well, they do, and I never know what to say . . . so today I asked him about the pub and *he* said it isn't a ghost . . ."

"*Ha!*" said Harry.

"Don't vicars believe in ghosts?" said Flora.

"He didn't say he didn't believe in them," said Valerie. "He said *this* one isn't a ghost. He said it's just a place memory . . ."

"The only problem with that," said Harry sarcastically, "is that places don't have minds – and no mind, no memory."

"Places do have atmospheres, though, don't they?" said Katherine.

"Like when you go into an empty house," said Flora, "and you can tell at once if it's got a happy atmosphere or a sad one or a frightening one."

"I'm glad to say I'm not that sensitive," said Harry. "Place memory!"

"Look, I'm just repeating what I was told," said Valerie. "According to Mr Foster, something that happens often enough, at the same time, in the same place, can get imprinted – so that it goes on repeating itself."

"Like a video?" said Lisa.

"Something like that, I imagine," said her mother. "He says nothing needs to be done about it because it has no more significance than an old photo."

"You go in there, don't you?" said Flora. "Have you ever seen it?"

"Never," said Valerie.

"Are you allowed upstairs, to look?"

"Oh yes, the upstairs has the Function Room and the Ladies."

"Can we come with you sometime?" said Flora. "Me and Lisa? We're allowed in if we're not drinking, aren't we?"

"Yes, we are," said Lisa. "I've sampled their Diet Coke a few times."

"I should warn you," said Harry, "that this apparition has only been seen once that anyone really knows about. Some visitors were asking Tom about it one evening when we were in. He put on a good 'oo-er' show for them, but he was a bit more honest with me afterwards. The last person to see it was his predecessor, and that was nineteen years ago."

"Photographs fade," said Katherine. "Maybe place memories do, too."

"That's taken all the fun out of that, then," said Flora.

"Cancel the Diet Coke," said Lisa. "We won't bother to stake out the upstairs landing."

"Not unless our neighbours break the ban and do their stuff," said Flora. "Then it's only fair we should be allowed to watch. We are locals, after all."

"It does seem to be rather their 'thing'," said Harry. "They exorcised Mrs Paxton's house as soon as they moved in."

"Never!" said Valerie. "I didn't know that!"

"So Tom told me."

"But there can't have been anything bad in *there*," said Katherine.

47

"There wasn't," said Lisa stoutly.

"Well, you wouldn't notice if there was," said Flora, making a statement rather than offering a criticism. "But I would have, and I agree, there wasn't."

"Perhaps for people like that," said Katherine doubtfully, "it's all part of the redecorating."

"That seems to suggest they really are as batty as we thought at first," said Valerie.

"Oh well," said Harry, "let's be fair. Tom may have got it wrong. He prefers talking to listening."

"Look at the time!" said Valerie suddenly, pushing back her chair. "We must go, the oven will be switching itself off in six minutes. Katherine, I'd ask you all to join us for lunch, but . . ."

"But you're going to eat some part of a dead animal," said Katherine cheerfully. "Don't worry, we have mushroom and onion pie and roast potatoes in the oven."

"And after we've eaten," said Flora, snatching up a teatowel and waving it above her head like a flag, "we'll reclaim our territory."

When it came to it, though, that was not as easy as it sounded.

· CHAPTER EIGHT ·

WHEREVER THE PEOPLE next door had been, they all got back at the same time, late in the afternoon. Katherine gave them half an hour, and then she and Flora went to knock on the back door. It was opened by the young man who had helped Ed with the screaming man, but although he smiled and invited them in, he wouldn't talk about the fence. "You'll have to ask Barbara," he said, and went off to find her.

They stood inside the back door, with the passage that led to the hall and the front room leading off to their right, and the passage that led to the kitchen leading off ahead, not quite sure if they were meant to penetrate further into the house or not. Time passed, during which two separate people they had never seen before wandered through from the front room to the kitchen, and although Katherine was willing to have the conversation with either of them, neither would discuss it. "You'll have to ask Barbara," they said, smiling.

"She's obviously busy," said Katherine, to the second of these people, a middle-aged man who looked as capable of understanding about the positioning of fences as anyone else. "There's no need to disturb her. I just wanted to know when you're going to put up the fence and if you realised that you've accidentally marked its position too far into my garden."

"I'm sure Barbara will come down and speak with you directly," said the man, and he went into the kitchen and closed the door behind him.

"Barbara really is the reigning monarch around here, isn't she?" said Flora.

"I can hear footsteps," said Katherine.

Barbara Marsh came down the stairs from one of the upper rooms. The young man was not with her. She looked tired and, when she was closer, they could see a tell-tale crease down the side of her face. She'd been lying down, resting.

"Sorry to keep you waiting," she said, as friendly as always. "Someone should have shown you into the front room. Do come along."

Even as she turned to lead the way, Katherine said, "No, really, we don't want to take up any of your time, it's just a very simple matter – a misunderstanding."

"Oh?" said Barbara, looking concerned.

Katherine had followed her habit of preparing an opening sentence, and even though the meeting hadn't started the way she'd expected, she found she couldn't launch into the subject without it.

"You've certainly cleared the garden," she began, and Flora added helpfully, "And the fence!"

Before either of them could say any more, though, Barbara Marsh interrupted. "Yes," she said, with unexpected passion, "and I pray it'll be granted to us to clear everything else that needs it, however much opposition we may meet."

Katherine, taken by surprise, could only stare, but Flora picked up the reference. "You want to clear the ghost out of the pub, don't you?" she said. "And they won't let you."

Barbara Marsh looked at her for a moment and then stretched out her hand and briefly touched the silver charm hanging around Flora's neck. "You and your brother are alike," she said, "both fascinated by the unpleasant things in life."

"It's a silver scorpion," said Flora, startled, putting her hand over it to protect it from disparagement. "Scorpio is my birth sign."

"Yes," said Barbara. Her voice was weary, almost wistful. "Forgive me," she said, obviously realising that her state was noticeable. "The service this morning was particularly exhausting – and I'm concerned about the situation at the pub."

"We won't keep you," said Katherine, feeling oddly out of her depth. "It's just . . ."

"Don't *you* find it distressing," said Barbara, "that the landlord of The Green Man is willing to give house-room to a demonic force, just for the entertainment of his customers?"

"Don't worry," said Flora. "The vicar says it's all right. He says it's only a kind of echo."

"I have a little booklet," said Barbara, "that might explain it to you in a very different way." She turned back to Katherine. "I have something important to ask of you," she said. "In fact I was going to come in and see you later." She smiled. "You've beaten me to it," she said, "so it's only fair that you speak first!"

"Oh, right," said Katherine and, having totally lost her carefully prepared speech, stuttered out something about the fence and its position.

"We shan't get around to putting the new one up until we've cleared all the rubbish from the garden," said Barbara, "but we have marked the correct place, I do assure you." Then, before Katherine had time to react or respond, she went on. "I understand from your son that you're planning a Hallowe'en Party," she said. "Please, could I ask you to reconsider?"

"Oh, don't worry," said Katherine, "we'll keep the noise down."

"It's only a kids' party," said Flora. "Just Jack and his friends, so it won't go on late."

"Oh, I don't object to parties," said Barbara, "far from it. But it's really terribly unwise to encourage anyone, especially young children, to dabble in the occult."

"No dabbling," said Katherine, "I guarantee. Just a light-hearted party, with dressing-up and games."

"We don't even do 'trick or treat'," said Flora, "because Mum says the neighbours mightn't like it."

"But if you think about it, it isn't really possible for anything connected with Hallowe'en to be lighthearted, is it?" said Barbara. "Hallowe'en is a relic of the Celtic Festival of the Dead. That's why your son was over here talking about vulture masks and skulls."

"Oh no," said Flora, surprised to find how indignant she was that Jack should be so misunderstood. "No, it isn't like that. Jack has a thing about vultures – he thinks people are unfair about them and he's always trying to make people understand them better and realise they do a good job. He's making a vulture mask because he thinks vultures are *nice!*"

Barbara looked at her for a moment. Then, "There are two separate conversations going on here," she said, "and at the moment the party seems to me to be the more urgent one." She reached out and touched the curved tail of the tiny scorpion once more. "Another time," she said to Flora, "I'd really be interested to hear you talk about these things. I'd like to understand what they mean to you."

"Sure," said Flora, slightly embarrassed.

The kitchen door opened and the middle-aged man leant around it so that his head and one arm were visible. "I've made a pot of tea," he said to Barbara, then withdrew his head and arm and closed the door.

"We must go," said Katherine rapidly, conscious of the weariness in Barbara's face and the protective look she fancied she had seen in the eyes of the tea-maker.

Barbara followed them the few paces to the back door and stood on the step. "Please reconsider," she said.

Katherine stopped on the path, Flora close behind.

"You think you're going to be in control of this party," said Barbara, "but you're not." She wasn't smiling now. "Hallowe'en is part of an ancient tradition which existed for hundreds of years before any of us were born. It's the one night of the year when evil is allowed free rein."

The early winter chill, which had first made itself felt the evening before, seemed to have gained a little strength today. Flora pulled the sleeves of her sweater down over her hands. A carrion crow, flying low over the garden to check if the extensive scything had ended the lives of any small mammals, croaked irritably at the intrusion of humans.

"You seem to be thinking of a much darker tradition than I am," said Katherine, slowly. "The tradition behind our kind of celebration is to ridicule and drive away evil. The children enjoy being mildly frightened, knowing there's no real danger."

As she was speaking, Barbara was shaking her head, but Katherine kept going. "In the old days," she said, almost as though she was telling a story, "when people believed there really were evil spirits abroad at Hallowe'en, they put pumpkin masks in the windows to ward them off. There was a very specific message, which was 'No need to call here, we have our own.' Even at its most dramatic this festival is not a celebration of evil, it is a celebration of triumph *over* evil."

Flora stood silent, watching the two women. There was a tension between them that was so strong that it even affected the way they stood. They stood very still, they spoke very quietly, very formally.

Barbara Marsh said, "Hallowe'en is a gateway in the wall between good and evil. You are planning to open the gate

– and Satan will make the most of the opportunity you offer."

"I think," said Katherine, and her voice was wintry, "that you're making a little too much of this. I guarantee that my children are not going to conduct Satanic rituals."

Unexpectedly, Barbara's expression softened and she reached out to touch Katherine's arm saying, as she did so, "I do hope you don't think I was suggesting such a thing!"

Katherine moved almost imperceptibly backwards, so that she was just out of reach of Barbara's hand. "I'm sure our party won't disturb you," she said, "in any way at all."

As she turned to go, Barbara said, "I've antagonised you, and I'm truly sorry. But please, ask yourselves why you want to do this thing, what is prompting you?"

"Goodbye," said Katherine, and she and Flora walked quickly back across the devastated garden, without looking behind them.

It was half-way through the following day before either of them remembered about the fence.

Later, Jack said he didn't know why Mrs Marsh didn't like skulls when she had dozens in her house.

"What *do* you mean?" said Flora.

"There's hers," said Jack, "and Ed's, and . . ."

"But they're *alive*," said Flora.

"I know that," said Jack. "Live people have skulls too. They have to, otherwise their heads would go all flabby."

Flora laughed, but Katherine was too shaken by the confrontation with Barbara to join in. "If we were going to do what she seems to *imagine* we're going to do," she said, "then she'd have reason to be worried. But how *can* she imagine it? What on earth does she think we are?"

Later still, Flora recounted the exchange to Lisa. "You're off the hook," she said. "I won't drag you to either of the other parties, I think we should stay here. I think Mum might need our support if next-door's going to get heavy."

"All right," said Lisa. "But . . . you don't think anything's going to happen, do you?"

"Not really," said Flora. "I just thought Barbara Marsh might come knocking on the door and we could take turns reassuring her, so Mum doesn't have to do it all."

"I didn't mean that," said Lisa. "I meant – don't laugh at me – I meant, what if Barbara Marsh is right?"

· CHAPTER NINE ·

I T WAS THE strangest Hallowe'en party any of them had
ever experienced.

It began in the smoky dusk of a clear, still evening. The
candle flames burned steady and straight inside the hol-
lowed-out pumpkins and did not flicker. One stood on the
window-table in the sitting room and grinned out at the
front gate. Another stood in the kitchen window and grinned out at the back garden. Around the pool, three more
exchanged wide, gap-toothed smiles with their own reflec-
tions in the shallow water.

Katherine said she couldn't see where to make a bonfire
without giving the newly planted tree a shock, so the rest
of the decorations were indoors. Rubber bats dangled from
the centre lights. Paper cut-out witches rode their broom-
sticks across the window-panes. Plastic spiders and beetles
crawled over the pumpkin pie, the bowls of crisps, the
cheese pasties and the witch's-hat chocolate cake. Tall cardboard skeletons, jointed at knee and elbow, hung on the
backs of doors and jigged their bony limbs whenever anyone
went in or out. A tape, on which Katherine, Flora and Lisa
had recorded a series of screeches and whines and cackles,
played endlessly behind a large cauldron-like bowl of water
with apples floating on its surface.

Grandma, having watched the preparations with little

comment — apart from saying that the witches should have had longer chins — retreated to her upstairs bedroom.

"She's lucky," said Flora. "Fifteen eight-year-olds aren't my idea of good company, either."

Jack's vulture mask was a triumph, even though he looked more like a miniature Aztec god than a carrion-eater, especially as his paper cloak was bright orange.

Katherine, with her long dark hair, a grey crêpe cloak stencilled like a spider's web and a wide-brimmed pointed hat, made a beautiful witch.

Tabitha, though not strictly the right colour for a witch's cat, wore an enormous black bow with a sequinned eye sewn onto each loop.

Flora, in orange leggings, was coping with a rather uncomfortable pumpkin shape of wire and orange crêpe paper suspended from her waist, topped by a green T-shirt and a full-face mask made of green pumpkin-leaf shapes.

"That cat looks weird," she said, in a muffled voice. "What's she meant to be?"

"She's meant to be weird," said Katherine. "It's all she'll wear and it's all I could think of, so it'll have to do."

Lisa, in a phosphorescent skull mask and a white crêpe-paper cloak, was posted at the gate well before the first guests were expected. Normally she wouldn't have minded at all. This time, though, she kept glancing nervously at the big house next to Flora's, willing the front door to stay closed.

When the sadness began, it wafted over her so gently that she didn't recognise it at first for what it was. When she did, though, she wondered why she hadn't felt it the moment she had taken up her position.

Last year, and the year before, she would have been out here, with Flora, and they would both have been keeping an eye on the same house. On those occasions, however, they would have been looking forward to the moment when the door would open and Mrs Paxton would come walloping out, clanging her walking frame against the porch wall because she was using it one-handed, the other hand being occupied in holding a plateful of something disgusting she had made especially for their party. One year it had been skull biscuits; the next it had been individual green jellies, turned out of a slug-shaped mould, with bits of green angelica-peel for feelers.

She had never stayed for the party itself, however much they had asked her to, but she'd never complained either, not even the year it had overflowed into her garden and become extremely noisy.

I wish I could believe you've gone on somewhere else, Lisa thought. If there was such a place as heaven, they'd be bound to let you in. They couldn't not.

She didn't remember that she had felt so cold, waiting by the gate in other years. She looked up at the hazy grey sky. A pigeon flapped heavily overhead, looking strangely ominous for such a silly bird, and from far behind her she heard the malevolent voices of the crows, arguing in the cemetery trees.

This was just the sort of peculiar light, Lisa thought, this early dusk on a dingy autumn day, that could deceive people into thinking they glimpsed witches riding on the up-currents or goblins swinging out of sight behind the branches of trees. It was a no-man's-land kind of light, between true light and true darkness, a boundary, a wall, perhaps – like the wall Barbara had described to Flora, with the doorway which could admit terrible things.

Then she thought, what if, instead of something awful coming out of the doorway, the whole world is drawn in through it?

She blew on her hands and scuffed her feet on the ground, partly to keep the circulation going, and partly to make contact with something solid and normal. I never think things like that, she muttered to herself, glaring at Mrs Paxton's old house to check that no one was watching her. It's getting dark because the sun's going down, that's all, and Flora says the crows are always noisy. And the only doors around here are the doors of the houses.

Then, to her relief, she saw three figures approaching from the far end of the road, the town end. Two small dinosaurs came first, one green with a thin tail, the other padded and purple, with triangular fins sticking up all along its back. They part-walked and part-skipped on their hind legs, and occasionally they pushed each other, staggered and ricocheted off the garden walls. Their giggles, though muffled inside their papier-mâché heads, carried well on the still grey air.

They were the kind of thing the phosphorescent ghost that was Lisa had expected to see. What she hadn't expected to see was the figure strolling along several paces behind them. "Ed," whispered Lisa to herself as she recognised him, and she stood in some confusion waiting for the inevitable confrontation, not knowing if she ought to feel more silly than evil, or more evil than silly.

She made a vague attempt at leaping out at the dinosaurs from behind the gate, but it wasn't much of a performance. They knew how to behave, though, and screamed and giggled rewardingly enough, then scampered up the path to the open front door, trying to tread on each other's tails.

Seconds later Ed was standing at the front gate. Far from being outraged, as she had feared, he was chuckling. "Hi, Lisa," he said. "You don't look too well."

"How did you know it was me?" Lisa mumbled through the mask.

"Lucky guess," said Ed.

Lisa stared out at him through the cardboard eye sockets. She suddenly realised she was desperately in need of his reassurance but didn't know how to ask for it. He raised his hand in a farewell gesture and began to walk on.

"Ed?" said Lisa, urgently.

He stopped. "Lisa!" he said, smiling.

"Ed," said Lisa, "it will be all right, won't it?"

Ed looked at her thoughtfully.

"We're just having ordinary party games," said Lisa, "and dressing up." She pointed down the road. A small masked demon was approaching in the company of a very human-looking woman, who was attempting to straighten out its horns as they walked. "We're not doing black magic or anything."

Ed looked faintly startled. "I should hope not!" he said.

"Well . . ." said Lisa, "I mean . . . we're not going to call up anything really evil by accident, are we? We're not putting the kids in danger?"

Ed stood aside as the demon ran up to Lisa and yelled "Yaaaaaah!" in what it thought might be a menacing voice.

Its mother said, "I'll be back sharp at nine, have a lovely time," smiled at Ed, laughed at Lisa, and walked back the way she'd come.

As the demon set off up the front path, Ed rested his hand briefly on its head, between the horns, and said to Lisa, "Do you think Jesus wouldn't protect one of these? Don't worry, Lisa, He sees behind the masks, He sees what's really there." Then he strode off, with a quick wave, and turned in next door.

"Thanks, Ed," said Lisa and for the next twenty minutes or so she relaxed and enjoyed herself.

The tone of the evening began to change when Katherine opened the door, in answer to three rings on the bell, and found Barbara Marsh on the step.

Their raised, though at first not angry, voices brought Lisa and Flora into the hall, followed not long afterwards by an assortment of miniature prehistoric beasts, devils, vampires and other exotic creatures.

Katherine, an earnest witch, was pleading with Barbara, who seemed to be near to tears.

"We're mocking evil," Katherine was saying patiently,

"bringing it down to a cosy level where children can be pleasantly scared in a safe and wholesome environment."

"This is the first step," said Barbara, interrupting her, "on a long and terrible road."

"I am not taking any steps," said Katherine. "I am giving a children's party."

"You're introducing these children to pagan and powerful forces," said Barbara, "as surely as if you were conducting occult rites. You are feeding dark energies, and you don't even know what you're doing, so you can't take any precautions at all."

Lisa felt her heart begin to beat rather too fast under her ghostly paper shroud. She took off the skull mask and said, "Ed told me it was all right."

Barbara looked from Lisa's face to the mask in her hand and back again. "If you want to ask anything," she said, gently, "anything at all, ask me. I'm always available, I'll always talk to you. The others are learning but their understanding is not fully developed yet."

She turned back to Katherine. Her face was very pale. "I don't know how to make you understand," she said, "that Satan himself is the guest of honour at this party of yours."

Flora said later that she had never seen her mother so angry. She didn't raise her voice, in fact she spoke very quietly, but her face was whiter than Barbara's and her hands were clenched. "Don't you dare tell me that!" she said. "If you want to talk about Satan, that's your business, but don't bring him to *my* doorstep."

Barbara put her hands up to her face and tears began to slip down her cheeks. "I'm not calling you evil," she said. "I'm saying you're misguided, I'm saying you don't understand, and I have to say it because I care about these children and the dangers . . ."

"Goodnight," Katherine cut in. "Please go so that I don't have to shut the door in your face – because if you don't go, then that's what I shall do."

61

Barbara turned away. "We'll pray for you," she said, and she almost ran down the path.

Two minutes later the singing started up, louder than usual, as though all the windows and probably the front door as well were wide open. Loud Gospel songs, punctuated by chanting, swept through the house in waves, and Katherine picked up Tabitha for comfort and held her close under her chin. "I mustn't feel angry with them," she said to Flora. "I really mustn't, because they think they're protecting us, they think they're putting out some awful fire for our sakes. But all the same I'd like to go in there and knock all their heads together."

The encounter, and the singing, had a curiously energising effect on the party. The braver children began to plague Katherine to let them 'conduct occult rites' and when she said she didn't know any, they began to invent their own, eventually running into the back garden and shouting out, "Good evening, Satan, do come in!" The more timid children became thoroughly unsettled and started complaining that the pumpkin lanterns were watching them. In fact some of them got so worked up that Flora had to blow out the candles and switch on the centre light.

"You and Lisa can judge the best costumes," said Katherine to Flora, "and hand out the prizes. That'll calm them down. I've got to go and read the riot act to Jack and his high-flyers – they really mustn't yell about Satan out there, it isn't fair."

Flora removed her mask and waddled off in search of the prizes, the pumpkin shape rocking from side to side as she walked.

Lisa took off her costume, gathered the nervous around her, and persuaded them to explain in detail how their outfits had been put together. It was a good move because the ones who had no idea still managed to make up a tale, and soon they were vying with each other to claim the most outlandish materials and to compete about whose parents had stayed up the latest the night before to produce the final creation.

"I wish I hadn't said anything to Barbara about Ed," she said to Flora quietly. "I think he was going to get into trouble."

"I think he's going to be made to toe the party line," agreed Flora, "but don't worry, he's old enough to take care of himself."

"I feel all unsettled now," said Lisa. "The fun's gone out of it."

"I think that was the idea," said Flora.

"You don't think we have . . . you know . . . invoked anything?"

Flora gave her a quick hug, not easy since she was still wearing her pumpkin outfit, and said, "Don't worry, ours is a nice house, ours is. I promise you, on my honour as a vegetable, Satan doesn't party here."

· CHAPTER TEN ·

L ISA LAY AWAKE in the dark. It was not solidly, suffo-
catingly dark, it was drearily dark. The pieces of furniture looked lumpish and faintly hostile – and somehow not
quite the right shapes. Bits of moonlight leaked in under
the curtains and formed puddles on the floor. The numbers
on the bedside clock glowed, like angry little red eyes.

She tried not to look at them because she preferred not
to know that it was coming up to midnight.

She could clearly remember what Ed had said at the gate,
and what Katherine had said about the party being innocent
and without hidden meanings, but she was no longer as
convinced as she had been. Now, with the slightly sulphur-
ous smell from smoking candles and singed pumpkins still
hanging around her clothes, where they lay on the floor by
the bed, it was easier to remember Barbara Marsh's urgent
voice talking about gateways – and about invitations being
accepted even if you didn't realise you'd issued them. She
wondered how many of Jack's small friends were having
nightmares.

When the first tiny noise came at the window, she thought
she'd imagined it. By the time the second noise came,
though, she was listening, and she knew it was real. Something had nudged at the pane and then slithered quietly
away.

Lisa lay still, staring at the curtains, made pale by the moon behind them.

It seemed a long time before it happened again and when it did, Lisa, grasping fistfuls of the duvet as if it could offer some protection, knew what it sounded like. It sounded as if something soft had brushed against the glass. Even though her bedroom was up on the first floor, and even though there was no sign of movement through the curtains, it sounded as though the corner of a cloak had flicked softly against the glass, in passing.

Lisa let go of the duvet and sat up in bed. "I do not believe," she whispered at the moonlit curtains, "in ghosts, I do not believe in evil spirits, I do not believe in magic, or auras, or vampires, or astrology. I do not believe in Satan, and therefore he can't be flying past my window."

She slid out of bed and stood on the floor.

She thought she had managed to stop the fear getting any worse. However, she had not managed to make it go away.

She stared at the dim shape that was her bedside lamp. She knew that if she switched it on, the room would become familiar and reassuring. On the other hand, the light could attract the attention of anything that might be outside.

"I know there is nothing outside," whispered Lisa.

But she didn't switch on the lamp.

She walked to the window, parted the curtains by the smallest amount possible, and looked through the narrow gap.

Down on the back lawn, a shadowy figure was swaying rhythmically from side to side.

Out in the garden, Flora stood first on one foot and then on the other, staring at Lisa's bedroom window and willing her to wake up. She thought she saw a tiny movement behind the curtains, but then some fragments of cloud began to cross the moon and break up its light and she couldn't be sure.

She picked up yet another handful of earth and grass from the edge of the lawn and threw it at the middle of the bottom pane. It hit the glass and slid down onto the windowsill, joining the little pile that had already formed.

This time, the curtains parted and Lisa stared out. Flora mimed pulling on jeans and a sweater and finally, with a great sweeping signal, indicated that Lisa should come outside quickly.

The three houses were dark and silent. There was no human sound to be heard. Over by the allotments an owl called twice, and somewhere on the far side of Mrs Paxton's old garden a fox gave a short, coughing bark. Apart from that, there was no non-human sound, either.

When Lisa appeared, sidling out of the kitchen door and closing it carefully, Flora signed to her to be quiet and led her between the houses and right out of the side gate onto the road before she spoke.

"Don't want to wake anyone," she whispered then.

"What are we *doing*?" said Lisa crossly. Her heart was still beating far more rapidly than was comfortable and the cold outside air was a shock.

"I gave you a fright, didn't I?" said Flora. "Sorry, but it *is* important. The Hallelujah Hall lot have gone up to stake out the cemetery, and Jack's followed. I have to go and bring him back, but I don't want to go on my own."

"What *are* you talking about," said Lisa, horrified.

"They think something's going to happen up there," said Flora. "Jack overheard them talking in the garden at the end of the party, and you know what he's like, it sounded like fun to him."

They were standing side by side, in the middle of the road, within the yellow smudgy circle made by the street lamp. The light seemed to offer a last little oasis of safety in an alien landscape. If the furniture in Lisa's room had looked hostile, the dimly realised shapes over in bandit-country looked downright menacing.

The moon was beginning to wane, and its light was not as bright as the patch on the curtain had suggested. It was possible to see enough to find the way but not to recognise details. Objects melted together as if they had taken off their daylight shapes to relax in sleep. The allotments seemed to be larger than usual and steeped in mystery, the geometrical formation of the town dump had become a small industrial complex, or even an oil refinery, and the trees of the distant cemetery looked like low storm clouds.

"I made him promise not to go," said Flora, "then just now I woke up and something made me check on him. He isn't in his room."

"Flora," hissed Lisa, "he's only *eight*."

"I know," said Flora. "Are you coming?"

Lisa looked at the fence opening. By day it was just a gap, something that wasn't there, a negative presence. By night, though, it seemed altogether more significant, a symbolic gateway dividing the normal from the monstrous.

"What do they think's going to happen?" said Lisa. The cold air stung her face and the back of her hands and she wished she had put on two sweaters.

"They think people are going to vandalise it," said Flora, with a certain amount of relish. "Conduct demonic rites."

"I don't want to see anything like that!" said Lisa, standing still, gripping Flora's arm. The street light washed all the colour out of their clothes and faces so that they became two small grey figures, entirely in keeping with the night.

"And I don't want Jack to see anything like that," said Flora.

"Oh," said Lisa. "No. Come on, then, it may not be so bad once we're through." She let go of Flora and they both crossed over the dividing line and into no-man's-land.

"I feel as if we should have a talisman," whispered Lisa, "to protect us."

"I'm wearing my Ankh," Flora whispered back, tugging at something on a chain around her neck.

"What's that?"

"Ancient Egyptian symbol of life."

"Is it all right to wear a symbol of life when you're going to a cemetery?" said Lisa. "Isn't it sort of insulting?"

"I wish you'd brought Goldie," said Flora.

"I didn't think of it. Shall I go back for her?"

"No, you might wake someone."

When they reached the end of the last allotment, they stopped. Then Flora leant forward and looked cautiously around the corner of the fence, over to the left where the ramshackle hut stood by the railway line. "No torchlight," she said. "No druggies over there tonight."

Lisa remembered the screaming man, and the memory of his nightmarish capering figure made her knees sag. She stood still, staring over at the long low wall which curved round the group of trees and said, "There are no lights at the cemetery, either. I don't think anyone's there. I don't want to go if we don't have to."

Flora hesitated, then she walked on. "They wouldn't show lights," she said, "not if they're setting an ambush. Anyway, I'm certain Jack's there." She looked back over her shoulder at Lisa and the watery moonlight glittered in her eyes.

Lisa, who couldn't remember when she had last been in bandit-country without the wide figure of Mother Grundy filling her vision and the sound of her current favourite tape occupying her hearing, was appalled at the realities of the dark landscape with its barely audible sounds, which suggested things flying, and crawling, and even killing and eating. She felt an unexpected flash of anger towards Flora. "You're enjoying this," she hissed.

"Life's meant to be enjoyed," said Flora. "You want to try it, you'd get a nice surprise."

"I can't enjoy *this*," said Lisa.

"Why not?"

"Because I'm frightened."

"You don't have to be," said Flora. "Nothing nasty's happening to us."

"No, but it might," said Lisa.

"What might be is only imagination," said Flora. "The reality is quite interesting, at the moment."

"You could have woken Katherine," said Lisa, "and she'd have come with us. You could have woken my parents and they'd have come in the car . . ."

"Then Jack would have been in trouble," said Flora.

"Not *that* much trouble!" said Lisa. "He's only a kid."

"But if we find him, there'll be no trouble at all," said Flora reasonably.

It was better in the open ground, beyond the tip, where it was obvious that no one could creep up on them, but then the cemetery loomed, its crumbling wall encircling the district of the dead.

Flora ran, bent double, right up to the wall and crouched down behind it. Lisa, rather than be left alone where she was, followed.

The big Victorian monuments, the slabs and table tombs and statues, were gathered in the original part of the cemetery, in the centre, among the trees. The small modern headstones and urns, among them the one which commemorated Mrs Paxton, formed an outer circle around them. Between the nearest of these and the wall where Lisa and Flora sheltered was a wide strip of neatly mown grass. There was no sign of movement, there were no lights, the tiny sounds were probably caused by owls and mice.

Flora nudged Lisa and pointed.

"What!" said Lisa. "What's happening?"

"Nothing," whispered Flora. "But why do you suppose so many of the table tombs have cracked tops, as though someone's just broken out?"

"They often do," said Lisa, "I've seen it in other places."

"Maybe the frost cracks the stone," said Flora, with interest, "and then the ground moves as the graves settle."

69

"I don't like it here," said Lisa. "It makes me think of death."

"You're so conventional," said Flora. "And why are you so twitchy? You always say you don't believe in anything, so what are you scared of?"

"People doing horrible things," said Lisa.

"Fair enough," said Flora, "but no one seems to be here, so if we can just find Jack . . ."

"We could call him," said Lisa, somehow not much liking the idea.

"We don't *know* there's no one else here," said Flora.

"The dead are here," said Lisa gloomily.

"But are they?" said Flora. "Mum says we're reincarnated and what's left is just our old shells."

"Dad says we go out like a light when it's switched off," said Lisa. "And there's nothing left." They stared at the dim graveyard in silence. "And Ed would say we go to Heaven," she added.

"Or to Hell," said Flora.

"I bet Barbara Marsh thinks we'll go to Hell," said Lisa, "after tonight."

"Hey, *look*," said Flora, whispering so urgently that her breath moved Lisa's hair.

"What?" said Lisa, grabbing her arm.

"Over there," said Flora, "as far to the right as you can see, look at that stone angel."

In the dim light and the chill air, the base of the distant statue was smoking with breath and a curved dark shape suggested a small crouching figure.

"Jack," mouthed Lisa, and they climbed the low wall together.

"Keep down," hissed Flora, as they ran.

"Don't scare him," Lisa hissed back, but too late. Even though Flora spoke Jack's name in his ear just before she put her hand on his shoulder, his scream of fright tore through the air, louder than seemed humanly possible.

70

Instantly, the cemetery was peopled with dark figures, each clinging to one of the funerary monuments, as though the day of judgement had come and Jack's cry had stood in for the last trump, calling the dead to rise from their graves.

· CHAPTER ELEVEN ·

FLORA SEIZED JACK'S right arm, Lisa seized his left, and they sandwiched him between them as the tall figures separated themselves from their gravestones and moved closer. Jack wriggled like an eel and demanded to be released, but neither of them heard what he was saying. They stared, their eyes trying to make some use of the thin moonlight, and saw that they were surrounded.

One of the figures, a hawk-faced middle-aged man in black jeans and a black roll-necked sweater, stood in front of them and glowered down at them.

"What are you doing here?" he said.

"Nothing," croaked Lisa.

"Walking the dog," said Flora, in a bright chatty voice, "but she's wandered off. I expect she's gone home on her own, so we'd better go too, or she'll bark to be let in and wake the whole neighbourhood."

"Are you telling me the truth?" said the man.

"I don't think they are," said a woman's voice from the darkness, "but I don't think we need worry about them."

Flora put her mouth close to Lisa's ear. "That's . . ." she began, but before she could finish, Barbara Marsh was beside the fierce-faced man, no longer wearing her white tracksuit, now as darkly dressed as he was.

She smiled at the three of them and spoke gently. "It's all right," she said. "You're quite safe, and I don't suspect

72

you of planning anything nasty out here. But I don't think you're walking the dog, either."

"All these people . . . ?" began Flora.

"We're all together," said Barbara. "We shall keep vigil until dawn. So far no one unpleasant has turned up – quite possibly *because* we're keeping vigil. Nevertheless, this is not a suitable place for you."

From being almost blinded by fear, they found they could see perfectly well, and although some of the faces were new to them, many, including Ed's, were familiar. The relief of discovering they had not fallen among warlocks made both Flora and Lisa temporarily giggly. Barbara, though, without actually commenting, managed to make it clear that she would prefer them to quieten down, and Jack was extremely annoyed with them.

"You hurt me," he complained, pushing up his sleeves and examining his arms for fingerprint bruises. "You didn't have to grab me, I wasn't going to run away."

"I'm sorry," said Flora, recovering herself. "I thought *they* were going to grab you – before I knew who they were."

"We came to rescue you," said Lisa, placatingly. "I didn't know I was holding you so tightly. I was scared, too, you know."

"*I* wasn't scared," grumbled Jack, "not until you jumped on me."

"Come along," said Barbara, speaking over her shoulder as she set off towards the cemetery gate. "It's time to go home."

The hawk-faced man made a move as if to protest, and Flora said, "It's all right, thanks, we'll take Jack."

"I want to see you safely indoors," said Barbara, firmly. Two of the younger members of the group volunteered to walk with them, and Flora repeated that it wasn't necessary. "We just came to get Jack," she said, "and we've got him. We'll go straight back. Where else could we go?" But

Barbara was adamant. "I'll be back," she said to the hawk-faced man. "I've met the parents already so I'm the best one to have a word."

Flora shoved Jack ahead of her as she followed Barbara out of the cemetery, by a rather more formal route than the one they'd used to get in. "We don't have to wake . . ." she began, but Barbara interrupted her. "How long had you been there?" she said to Jack. "We didn't hear you or see you."

"I can be very quiet," said Jack, proudly.

"I shall be glad when this night is over," said Barbara, and she strode the rest of the way through bandit-country just ahead of them, without speaking again until they reached Flora's gate. Then, "I shall take you home first," she said to Jack, "as you're the youngest."

"Thank you for bringing us back," said Flora, formally, "but it's best if we go in through the kitchen without disturbing Mum."

"I'm sorry," said Barbara, and she looked as though she really might be, "but I'm afraid I have to ring the bell and deliver you properly. I think it's important that your mother knows where you were."

"We'll tell her in the morning," said Flora. "I don't want her woken now, it's after twelve-thirty."

But Barbara was already walking up the path. "I'm responsible for you until I put you in the charge of another adult," she said.

Flora skipped in front of her, so that she reached the front door first, leaving Lisa and Jack to trail behind. "Look," she said, very serious now, facing Barbara, blocking her path, "you needn't feel responsible. It wasn't your fault that Jack followed you."

Barbara Marsh stood for a moment, watching her. Then, "I'm aware whose fault it was," she said, "and the Good Lord knows I'm not here to get any of you into trouble." In one quick movement she reached behind Flora and rang the bell. "I have to do this," she said. "This is too important to ignore."

Flora looked at Lisa and made a face. "I tried," she said, and reached out to put one arm around Jack. "Mum's going to be furious."

"She's never *that* cross," said Jack, sleepily.

"I didn't mean with you," said Flora.

"I think I'll go home," said Lisa, but no one seemed to hear. She stayed where she was.

Katherine responded to the bell so rapidly that she was still half-asleep when she opened the door. She looked startled and confused.

Barbara Marsh began to speak at once. "I found them up at the cemetery," she said, "and I don't like to think what might have happened if they'd met the kind of people who usually go to cemeteries on this night of the year."

Katherine screwed up her eyes, pushed her hair off her face and looked at Flora.

"Jack followed the Hallelujah Hall lot up there," Flora said, briefly, manoeuvring him over the doorstep and shoving him gently at Katherine "and we went to bring him back. That's all. No sweat."

"Are you all right?" said Katherine, to Jack, taking him by the shoulders and looking anxiously into his face.

"Course I am," said Jack.

"Well, scoot on up to bed, then," said Katherine, "and we'll talk about it in the morning."

It was a measure of how tired Jack was that he went at once, remarking wistfully as he plodded up the stairs, "I didn't see anything scary – except Flora and Lisa."

"I know you won't be pleased to hear it," said Barbara Marsh, "but I have to point out that this is the sort of thing that stems from Hallowe'en parties. If only you could see that there are steps, and that one step leads to the next. You encouraged the first step, the next step had to follow."

"Now just hang on a minute," said Katherine.

75

"I did try to let you do this the quiet way," said Flora to Barbara.

"Flora tells me Jack was following *you*," said Katherine. "What's that got to do with the party?"

"Satan has his human helpers," said Barbara, as if that answered the question, "and desecrating graves is one of their nasty habits."

"And our party is supposed to be responsible for that?" said Katherine, snapping the words out almost as though they were pellets.

"Of course not," said Barbara, "but it *is* responsible for these children deciding to go up there and join in."

"Jack wasn't going to join in anything," said Flora. "He thought you were going to watch for vampires and grave robbers and it sounded like fun to him. He's eight years old, it's not an unusual reaction."

"It isn't a healthy reaction, either," said Barbara.

"Well, I can tell you," said Katherine, "that my children never did anything so unhealthy as hang around a cemetery at midnight before you moved in. Never. It wouldn't have occurred to them. And we have a Hallowe'en party every year."

"I understand why you're angry," said Barbara. "It's because I make you confront things you don't want to confront. No one wants to think about cemeteries being vandalised, yet it happens. You read your papers tomorrow morning and tell me if it hasn't happened somewhere."

"It's never happened here," said Katherine.

"I'm glad," said Barbara, "but you don't cancel your insurance just because your house hasn't burned down, do you?"

"I'm too tired for this conversation," said Katherine. "I think it's your fault they were up there, but I don't think you meant it to happen, and you did bring them straight back. Let's not fight. We're both on the same side, really."

Barbara Marsh turned away from the doorway, which

now sheltered Katherine and Flora, side by side. She put her hand on Lisa's shoulder and steered her away from them, down the path. That was why Lisa was the only one who heard her say, quite softly and quite sadly, "No, I don't really think we are."

"Lisa," said Katherine, her voice, though quiet, carrying clearly down the path. "Come in with us and nip over the fence. No need to disturb anyone."

Lisa stepped out from under Barbara's hand and looked up into her face, which was all grey in the orange light from the street lamp. "My parents'll be really annoyed if you wake them," she said, "and they won't listen to a thing you say. I'll tell them all about it tomorrow, I promise."

Barbara spread her hands to show that Lisa was free. "All right," she said and she gave a funny little smile. "I don't need to make any more enemies tonight."

Lisa didn't know why she suddenly felt so sorry for Barbara. It had something to do with the fact that they were both outside, in the cold and the dark, while Katherine and Flora and Jack were secure in their house; and something to do with the fact that although she could see why Katherine was so angry, she could also see that Barbara really did care about their safety.

"We really and honestly weren't doing anything evil at the party," Lisa said. "You don't have to worry about us, I promise you."

"I'll believe you," said Barbara. "But if you truly want to reassure me, promise me something else: promise to come to one of our meetings, just to give us a fair hearing. There's a big one on Sunday afternoon. Will you be there?"

"Are you coming, Lisa?" said Katherine, leaning out of the front door.

"Yes," said Lisa and, glad of the chance to avoid making a decision, she turned to go back up the path, but before she had taken the first step she heard Barbara, behind her, say, "Good. Thank you."

"Oh," said Lisa, turning, "I meant 'yes' to Katherine . . ." but Barbara was already at the gate, and if she heard, she gave no sign of it.

"What was that all about?" said Flora, as Lisa walked into the hall.

"She thinks I've agreed to go to one of their meetings," said Lisa. "I didn't mean to, but she thinks I've promised."

Flora laughed, "Don't worry," she said, "you'll wriggle out of it."

"I don't wriggle out of things," said Lisa, stepping into the warm hall with some relief. She was tired and cross and well aware that she still had to get into her own house without waking her parents. "I do all kinds of things."

"No," said Flora, who was tired too, and in a mood to be picky, "you duck all kinds of things."

"I came tonight!"

"Yes," said Flora, relenting. "Thanks. You're a good mate. I'm just saying that when it comes to anything you know involves more than three people, you panic."

· CHAPTER TWELVE ·

NATURALLY, LISA WENT to the meeting.

    She told her parents she was going to watch a video with Carrie, almost the only school friend, other than Flora, she ever visited. She didn't tell Flora anything at all. She wanted to be free to stay at home if she changed her mind at the last minute. In fact, she very nearly did. When she looked at the leaflet Barbara had given her, she saw that the meeting was not being held in Mrs Paxton's house but in a hotel at the opposite edge of town, two bus rides away.

The hotel looked larger than it was because it stood in the centre of its own garden. Its name, Ellesdon Court, was still written up above the main door, but the sign which had once stood by the gate had collapsed into a bush and been replaced by one that said FOR SALE. The big double doors were folded back, open, but some of the downstairs windows were shuttered on the inside, and although nothing looked actually broken, there was a slight air of dereliction about the place.

Lisa, who had managed to get herself that far by thinking, I'm only going to look, I don't have to go in, found its appearance thoroughly unsettling. She had just decided to cross the road and catch the first of the two buses home, when a car horn hooted briefly and the Cadillac swept past her into the drive. Several people got out and Ed, who was the first, hurried straight over to her and said, "Hi! Isn't Flora with you?"

"No," said Lisa, not entirely sure why she was irritated by the question.

"I didn't see you leave, or I'd have given you both a lift," said Ed. "Barbara didn't want us to call for you in case it seemed we were putting pressure on you."

"That's OK," said Lisa.

I'm stuck now, she thought, I have to go in. She remembered something Katherine once said: sometimes the only way out of something is through it.

Ed walked at her side, talking cheerfully. She could hear Barbara's voice coming from behind her, and ahead, inside, there were other voices, other people, quite a crowd. I could turn and run, thought Lisa, but it would look so silly, how would I explain? I have to go through this, I have to go through these doors, and through all these strangers, and through this meeting, and when I come out the other side I will be free.

A sudden tremendous press of people behind her suggested that a bus had just arrived, and above their voices she could hear the slamming of more car doors out on the drive.

The room they were all jostling into had obviously once been the ballroom. It had long bright windows, a polished floor, and a heavy-looking chandelier which glittered dangerously overhead.

Ed disappeared in the crowd, she could no longer hear Barbara, everyone was taller and older than she was, and there were so many of them, all on the move, all talking, all manoeuvring her to and fro, back and forth, that she felt like a small piece of rubbish caught up in a tidal river.

Wherever she stood there always seemed to be two or three people pushing her gently aside to get by. Sometimes she thought she recognised someone she had seen going in or out next door, but always they moved away before she could be sure. She lost all sense of which part of the room she was in. The noise made her giddy. Plastic-seated metal-legged chairs scraped and clattered as they were lifted from their stacks and moved about, chattering voices rose and fell in surges, and the great sheets of glass in the windows caught the sounds and threw them back on themselves until they had nowhere to go but up, where they annoyed the chandelier and set its glass beads chinking one against another.

The heating was on and it was stuffy already. Lisa felt herself breathing fast, her mouth open. I won't be able to go through this and out, she thought; or possibly she spoke the words aloud, the blurry hum of sound had become so unreal that she couldn't tell if any of it was coming from her or not. I don't belong here, I have to get out, I have to find the door, but I think the door has disappeared. I think there are only bodies, and noise, and huge closed windows.

"Are you on your own?" said a woman's voice, cutting clearly through the clatter.

Lisa managed to nod.

"Come and sit by me," said the woman, and she lowered herself onto one of the chairs and pulled Lisa down beside her. Within seconds almost everyone else sat, also, and the room took on its normal shape again.

It turned out that in all the apparent chaos people had actually been setting chairs in neat rows, with a centre aisle, and also a wide side aisle on the door side. The door was now clearly visible, and slightly open, and Ed and Barbara were visible, too, up on the small stage at the front. Lisa looked at the woman beside her, who smiled back at her, an ordinary, calm smile. Perhaps I can go through it after all, thought Lisa, and this time she definitely did not speak aloud. Perhaps I can.

Even so, it was a while before she could pay attention properly, and she hardly heard Barbara's opening words. What she did hear, though, was the singing.

81

Quite suddenly, everyone stood at once, Lisa with them, more or less borne up by the people on each side and in front and behind. The woman next to her gave her a word-sheet, and at first she just held onto it, but later, she didn't know how much later, she was aware that she was holding it up, reading from it, singing with them.

The singing – the chanting – on that scale, with that number of voices, had a resonance she had never experienced before. And while the unfocused noise at the beginning had been nightmarish, this sound, which was ordered, concerted, joyful, was entirely different.

She was not conscious of it being loud, although it must have been; she was aware only that it was powerful, rich, deep – and not deep in tone but deep in quality, deep like the roots of old trees, deep like the rocks which are a part of the earth's structure, deep like the centre of all things.

She seemed to hear it not only in her ears but in her skull and in her bones. If her bones had been hollow like a bird's they could not have held more of the sound.

She was swaying with the singing, because everyone was swaying with the singing, and when the singing stopped and Barbara began to speak again they went on swaying, because Barbara spoke in rhythm, just as they had sung in rhythm, and the beat and the rhythm were in tune with the beat and the rhythm of the life in all of them, the breath in the lungs and the blood in the veins.

Not only did Lisa no longer want to leave, she would not have known how to, any more than a limb knows how to detach itself from the body. She swayed with them not because she chose to, but simply because that was what she did.

Barbara, all in white, spoke without a microphone, and her voice carried around the hall as strongly as the singing.

"We are the Lords of Creation," she said. "We are made in God's image. But we don't always behave that way. Sometimes we are greedy, or spiteful, or cruel, or fearful.

We ignore God's plan for us. We bring grief to the heart of Jesus, who suffered for us, and died for us, out of pure love."

She paused, but the rhythm was powerful and did not wish to be broken, so the people in the hall instinctively filled the silence. "Hallelujah!" they shouted, and for the first time Lisa, on the inside now, understood why they did it, understood why it was necessary.

"But we don't have to be shackled by fear and guilt and bad feelings," said Barbara.

"If we are that way it's because we choose to be, even though we may not know we're choosing it.

"If we are that way, it's because we allow ourselves to be that way, even though we may not know we are allowing it.

"If we are that way, it is because we permit Satan to bind us with negative thoughts and with negative acts that take away our power, that take away our energy, that take away our ability to stand tall – and to be proud – and to be free – as God created us."

"Hallelujah!" they all said, and Lisa said it too, pleased that this time she'd known it was coming, pleased to be able to shout and release some of the energy that was building up in her.

Then came the chanting –

> "Jesus loves me – Praise the Lord.
> Jesus is with me – Praise the Lord."

Then came the strong happy Gospel songs that swung along, some people clapping in time to the pulse, some people stamping to swell the beat. The wooden floor danced under their feet, the echoing windows magnified the glory of the singing, the beads of the chandelier shimmered in celebration.

Lisa felt she was outside time and outside space, there was no room in her mind for anything except what was happening here and now, Barbara speaking, then the chanting, then the singing, and Barbara speaking again, always saying the same things, though sometimes in different ways.

"You were created free and good and powerful. This is the Truth. Why listen to the lies of Satan, Satan who binds you with the love of material possessions, Satan who binds you with fear and despair, Satan whose noise and clamour stops you hearing the voice of Jesus?

"If you are held by Satan it is because you are asleep. And if you are asleep, I will wake you!

"If you are deceived by Satan it is because you are his prisoners. And if you are prisoners, I will free you!

"Shake off Satan's bonds, shut your ears to Satan's voice, put your trust in Jesus and He will show you the way. Listen to Him and He will tell you that He loves you, that He is waiting to help you, that if you ask Him, He will free you from all the tangles and all the muddle that Satan has built around you."

Extraordinary things began to happen. A man hurried to the front, calling out something that Lisa couldn't catch, and Barbara leant down from the platform and rested her hands briefly on his head. A quietness came over the room, so that everyone heard him give thanks for being cured, and then there was applause and a hymn of praise. There were others, too, one of them a woman leaning heavily on a walking stick, who had to be led up to the platform by a helper, but who walked slowly back carrying the stick, her helper still at her side but no longer holding her arm.

Lisa, hearing the words, feeling the singing, was aware that something extraordinary was happening to her, also.

She felt herself taken apart, very gently, very delicately; taken all to pieces and then put together again in a different form. Each of the individual and familiar parts of her mind remained – all her thoughts, her memories, her ideas – but they were carefully separated from each other and then put back together in a different pattern, the right pattern, the pattern they had been designed to form. They fitted into this new pattern in a way that had not been possible before. They were at the same time more comfortable and more exciting. Facets that had once scratched against each other were now turned around, so that their smooth surfaces met and their angular surfaces faced outwards and caught the light.

As the service went on, she knew that something immense was happening outside her as well as within – someone was watching, watching everyone but especially watching her.

Someone both near and far, vast enough to contain the universe and small enough to be contained in a single seed, splendid beyond belief and gentle beyond measure, was watching and waiting, as patiently as a gardener waits for a plant to grow.

Two emotions began to build inside her, an almost over-whelming sadness to do with martyrdom and agony and death, and an intensity of love beyond anything she had even glimpsed before.

She didn't know if she could bear it. She felt a desperate need to share it with someone but knew that it was beyond her to begin to explain it. Then she looked up at Barbara and Ed on the platform and saw that they were feeling it too.

The woman beside her put her arms around her and hugged her. She felt it, Lisa knew she felt it. All over the room people were hugging each other, some were crying, some were laughing – they all felt it, they all understood, the whole roomful was in the same wild, extraordinary state.

"Jesus loves you!" said the woman who had hugged her, brushing the tears from Lisa's face with her hand. "Jesus loves you!"

"Hallelujah," said Lisa. And then she fainted.

· CHAPTER THIRTEEN ·

Lisa wouldn't say anything until she was with Flora
in her room, the door safely closed against Katherine
and Jack. Even then she couldn't start at once but sat without speaking on the edge of the chair, on top of a pile of
clothes. She sat lightly, not as though she was tense but as
though every muscle in her body, from the largest back
muscle to the tiniest face muscle, was engaged, alert, alive.
There was an excitement about her, but at the same time
she seemed completely self-contained, totally in control. She
looked almost as though she might fly.

Flora settled herself cross-legged on the bed and waited.
She realised that for the first time, ever, she had no idea
what Lisa was going to say or do. She watched with interest
as Lisa, still silent, leant forward to fiddle with the pile of
ear-rings and pendants on the dressing-table, disentangling
slender hooks from silvery shapes, separating a crescent
moon from the claws of a scorpion, the points of a star
from the curved tail of a dragon, an Egyptian Ankh from
the spread wings of a tiny bat.

She had begun to play with the little ornaments to give
herself time to decide what to say, but as she touched them
she began to be more and more fascinated by them. The
longer she looked at them the sharper was her realisation
that although she had seen them all before she had never

paid them any attention, had never noticed how delicately they were made, with what perfect detail.

She raised her head and looked past Flora and through the bedroom window behind her. Outside was the familiar shape of the large sycamore tree that grew at the edge of Mrs Paxton's old garden. Lisa knew there was nothing particularly remarkable about it, there were sycamores all over town. Now, though, even though she was seeing it through streaky glass, it did look remarkable. The solid trunk, dark against the clarity of the autumn sky, all the thousands of leaves that had already fallen, the few hundred that still clung on, the multiplicity of winged fruits that spun away to sow tiny saplings in unsuitable places in all the surrounding gardens – all that came from nothing more than a single seed, fed by earth and rainwater. It seemed astonishing.

"What *is* it?" said Flora, who had tried hard to be sensitive and patient, but couldn't keep it up. "You came from somewhere in the Cadillac, I saw you get out of it. What happened?"

"I went to the meeting," said Lisa, and for the first time since she had come in she looked directly at Flora with eyes that were brighter, more awake, than Flora had ever seen them. "Oh – Flora – it was *so wonderful!* It's changed the whole world – things even *look* different – I can't tell you – I don't know how to explain."

She had always intended to talk to Flora about it, but she had imagined herself doing it in quite a different way. She had supposed she would say something like, '*You* said I wouldn't go, but I did, so there!' She was amazed at how childish and pointless that sentence seemed to her now.

"I don't know about 'things' looking different," said Flora, "but you're different!"

"I can't talk about it and I can't not talk about it," said Lisa, "and I can't go home yet because I can't tell them. Dad'll make a joke of it and Mum'll disapprove and I can't stand it if anyone tries to spoil it."

87

"I won't spoil it," said Flora, "but you don't have to tell me if you don't want to." She was sure that was the right thing to say, but she was not at all sure she could bear it if Lisa kept quiet.

She need not have worried, though, because once she had begun to speak Lisa couldn't stop. She told Flora how weird it had been at the beginning and how totally it had changed. She remembered the words of the chants, and if she tried hard enough she found she could remember the words of some of the songs as well. She didn't have to try to remember the fiery emotions that had blazed in her because they were unchanged. So was the sense of being different, re-formed.

"And there were people there I recognised," she said. "You remember the screaming man?"

Flora made a face.

"He was *there*," said Lisa, "with his girlfriend, you know, the one I heard crying? She looked so happy, and he looked normal, he really did. He was white and thin and sort of ill-looking, because it takes ages to get better from something like that, but he wasn't out of his head any more. He's in some special drugs place, Ed said, drying out or whatever they do, but they let him out for the afternoons, and he was there, and singing, and not angry with her any more. And everyone we've ever seen go in next door was there. And you know that very quiet one, who's in the Post Office? She was there, and she was singing and waving her arms – she looked quite different, she looked *great*."

"You look great," said Flora. "Even your hair looks pleased with itself."

"Perhaps it'll go red in favourable light, now," said Lisa, running her hands through it until it stood out from her head, "like yours goes green. But the point *is*, I don't mind if it does or not, none of that matters. I thought I'd feel silly for fainting, but none of that mattered either, because other people fainted, too, and some of them cried and some of them laughed – Flora, it sounds daft, it sounds ridiculous, but if you'd *been* there . . ."

"I'd have done all three," said Flora, and she began to giggle, and Lisa began to giggle, too, because Flora laughing never spoiled anything. Flora had always laughed with, not at.

"And then Ed and Barbara drove me back," said Lisa, "and the others from next door came in other cars, but everyone else just went home. There were people from all over, they'd come by bus and bike and everything. And Barbara, when she's talking on the platform, she just looks beautiful, and Ed of course looks beautiful too, and they're so different, still themselves but so different! And I didn't want to get out of the car because I didn't want the feeling to end, but they said it never will end, it's part of me now – and I'm part of it."

"You always were part of it," said Flora, "you just didn't know it!"

"You're really pleased, aren't you?" said Lisa. "I wasn't sure if you would be."

"I am," said Flora, "of *course* I am, why wouldn't I be?" and she put the palms of her hands on the bed and pushed until she was bouncing up and down, still in a cross-legged position, and laughing because she knew how stupid it looked and because Lisa was laughing, too. "I've been trying to tell you about it ever since I knew you, but I could never get your attention."

"But you don't believe it," said Lisa, astonished, now.

"I do," said Flora, "I always have. I can't imagine how anyone doesn't, it seems so obvious to me."

"But you don't believe in God," said Lisa, "and you don't believe in Jesus-Christ-the-Son-of-God-who-died-for-our-sins. I know you don't."

"That's not exactly the way I see it," said Flora, "but it's all the same thing. We're each given it in the way we can understand it best. You don't see it the way I do, you see

89

it the way they do, but that doesn't matter, we both know what we mean."

"But it's the Truth," said Lisa, "what they were saying today. There can't be more than one Truth!"

"No, but there's more than one way of perceiving the truth," said Flora. "We each get directions in our own language. After all, that's only polite – and practical. Who'd have thought it'd take Gospel songs to get through to *you!*"

Quite suddenly she climbed off the bed, pulled Lisa to her feet, and began to dance her round the room. "You can go next door," she said, "and sing their songs, and I'll go on communicating in my own way, and we'll both be heard. Hey, do you think it was an accident they moved into that house? Maybe they were guided to it – just for you!"

"I don't know what to do about my parents," said Lisa, suddenly going rigid so that they both stopped and were still. "I don't want to tell them, not yet anyway."

"Then don't," said Flora simply, releasing her and clambering back into her cross-legged position on the bed.

"But maybe I have to. It's not the sort of thing you're meant to keep secret, is it, you're meant to tell everyone."

"I should think you'd be allowed to get used to the idea yourself, first," said Flora. "That seems fair."

"I don't know," said Lisa, and some of the happiness seemed to go out of her. "You won't say anything to Katherine yet, will you?"

"I won't say anything to anyone," said Flora.

"You promise?" said Lisa.

"I promise," said Flora. "It's for you to tell. But I'm glad you told me."

"Do you think they'd mind," said Lisa, "if I went in next door, before I go home, and asked if it's all right to keep it secret, just for a while?"

"They can't mind," said Flora, grinning at her, "you're part of them, now."

Lisa grinned back. "Yes," she said, "yes, I suppose I am,

aren't I?" Then she laughed because she was surprised how rich and comfortable that made her feel. "I'm part of everything, now!"

· CHAPTER FOURTEEN ·

A S SHE TURNED in at the gate, Lisa realised this was the first time she had seen the house clearly as it was now – as the focal point of a modern religious community – and not as Mrs Paxton's old home.

It wasn't that she had forgotten Mrs Paxton, or stopped loving her; it was that she had at last understood that the owner had moved on and so, in its own way, had the house.

Like the sycamore, the house seemed remarkable. Before, it had looked friendly and a bit muddled. Now, although nothing had changed outwardly, not even the window curtains, it looked ordered, important.

And it wasn't only the house and the tree that had changed without changing. The same thing had happened to her own body. She had been aware of it as she went in to Flora's house. She was more aware of it now. It was no longer the wrong shape, it was no longer imperfect – neither was it perfect. It just was, it was itself. She felt a tremendous sense of relief. She didn't have to fret about it any more. That's that, then, she thought, satisfied. I can think about other things, now.

What she wanted to do was to go into the house, be hugged by everybody she met, ask for some advice on how best to speak to her parents, and find out when the next prayer meeting would be held. It didn't occur to her that there might be a problem with any of that.

As she reached the front door it opened, and Ed was there, but he was not looking out, he was stooping down fiddling with something on the floor.

"Hallo," said Lisa.

Ed looked up at her and then straightened. He was lifting a suitcase, Lisa saw. He smiled at her but he looked distracted. "Did you want me?" he said.

"I wanted to ask something," said Lisa, thrown by the change in his manner.

"This is your second home," said Barbara's voice, from far back in the hall. She hurried into view, smiling. "Come in," she said.

Lisa stood aside to let Ed pass her. He hesitated, looking down at her, and she assumed he was going to tell her where he was going. When he didn't speak, and when Barbara called again, quite firmly, "Come in, Lisa," she felt confused.

Ed hitched the case into a more comfortable grip, and reached out his other hand to touch her shoulder, very briefly. "Trust in the Lord," he said, and he did not smile, he looked very serious.

"Yes," said Lisa, uncertainly.

Ed nodded, but still he didn't smile. "Remember that power belongs to Him and only to Him," he said, looking very intently at her. He looked, it seemed to Lisa, as though he very much wanted her to understand something extra from the words. Then he turned abruptly and hurried down the path.

Lisa stared after him. Whatever he had wanted her to understand, she had not understood it.

She looked to Barbara. "Where's Ed going?" she said.

Barbara closed the front door without speaking and gestured that Lisa should go into the sitting room. It was extraordinarily bare. The grey carpet was still on the floor but there was hardly any furniture — just chairs, mostly upholstered ones with wooden arms, though a few were plastic and metal-legged like the ones at the meeting. There was also a low table, and on the table there were about twenty Bibles, not big old church Bibles, but small plain school Bibles. That was all.

Lisa looked around, puzzled. She realised she had expected to see holy pictures, a cross, maybe even a small altar. She glanced at Barbara, wondering if perhaps this room was not finished yet and all that sort of thing was somewhere else.

Barbara seemed to know what she was thinking. "We have no religious images here, Lisa," she said. "That's idolatry. The Bible warns us against idolatry."

If Lisa thought of an idol, she pictured a primitive wooden statue, or an enigmatic stone head. "But a cross isn't an idol," she said, mystified. The songs had not only been hymns of praise, some of them had told the story that Lisa had heard before but never really listened to. She felt she wanted to remind Barbara of something, to say to her, "God died on a cross, in human agony, to save us all," but she stopped herself, knowing that it was hardly possible that Barbara could have forgotten.

Barbara sat down in one of the wooden-armed chairs and signalled Lisa to sit in another. They were not quite opposite each other. There was no atmosphere in the room at all, none of the surging excitement of the meeting.

Lisa thought, that was the Introduction, now I have to do Chapter One, and it's going to be harder. Her pleasure that she had understood this for herself made up for the slight disappointment she was beginning to feel.

"Is Ed all right?" she said.

"If we use a symbol to help us to pray," said Barbara, ignoring the question, "then very soon we find we are praying to the symbol itself. It's very dangerous. And it's just what Satan wants. He attacks in many ways, some of them very cunning, and one of his most subtle ploys is to deceive people into thinking they are Christians when they are not."

Like Ed, Barbara seemed to be trying to tell her something particular, something Lisa couldn't quite grasp.

"Is Ed coming back?" she persisted.

"Satan likes to divide people," said Barbara, and she smiled at Lisa, a little wearily, "but we stand firm. Ed will understand eventually. I pray it will be before it's too late."

"But why has he gone?" said Lisa. She would have preferred to talk to Ed. Barbara was the leader, and friendly though she was there was a power about her, a strength of will, that made it seem inappropriate to relax too much in her presence. Ed was different, easy-going, approachable.

"Don't worry about Ed," said Barbara, quite firmly. "What did you want to see me about? Was it something particular, or did you just want to talk? It's quite all right, if you just want to talk."

"I haven't told my parents yet," said Lisa. "I haven't been home since the meeting."

"Won't they be concerned about you?"

"I told them I was going to a friend. They'll expect me back soon, but not just yet." She looked Barbara straight in the eyes. "I lied," she said.

"You must pray for forgiveness," said Barbara, but she didn't look too shocked or cross. "Your parents are not likely to be very sympathetic to this, are they?" she said. "Not at first, anyway."

"No," said Lisa. "Do I need to say anything?"

Barbara leant back in her chair and closed her eyes for a moment. The room became very quiet. Lisa could hear her own belt creaking as she breathed.

Then Barbara opened her eyes and sat forward again. "When it's all over," she said, "those who are not saved will go to eternal damnation in Hell. If you love someone, if you love your parents, you must want them to be saved."

She smiled, then, but quietly, not the way she had at the meeting – it seemed some of her energy had been used up and had not yet regenerated.

95

"On the other hand," she said, "with some people, and I suspect with your parents, if you go at them head-on they become defensive and close their minds and you can find you've done more harm than good. It seems to me the best approach for you may be to let a little time pass, let them see how much happier you've become, how much more you're getting out of life. And when they notice this, and remark on it, then you can tell them why. It's important to approach everyone differently, in the way that's best for them."

"That's what Flora says," said Lisa, nodding.

"You've talked to Flora?" said Barbara. She seemed surprised, not entirely pleased.

"Yes. As soon as I got back." Lisa felt her own face spread into a smile as she remembered it. "She was *really* happy for me," she said.

"Try to bring Flora with you, next time," said Barbara. "She's at risk. Probably more at risk than many unbelievers."

"Oh no," said Lisa, "Flora does believe, in her own way."

"There is only one way to believe," said Barbara and she looked at Lisa with such intensity that Lisa felt she must be seeing right through to the inside of her mind. She found herself hoping it was tidy in there.

"There is no middle ground," said Barbara, "that is what Ed chose not to understand. Lisa, you must know this, because it is vital, literally vital for you to know it. We are all born into Satan's Kingdom. The earth and everything that is in it and everyone that is on it, is his. We are all his – unless we positively choose to belong to Jesus. That is what 'Witnessing' means. We have to stand up, in the face of Satan, and choose Jesus."

"But Jesus died for us," said Lisa, so startled that it didn't occur to her that she was contradicting Barbara. "He died for our sins – we are saved!"

"Oh, Lisa," said Barbara. "It didn't end there. While the

world exists there can be no endings. The battle goes on — and it is a mighty battle — for the souls of humanity. We have to fight, and we have to make very sure that we are fighting on the side of Jesus, that we have not been beguiled and deceived and misled into fighting in Satan's army by mistake."

She pushed back the wooden-armed chair and stood up. "Now we'll pray," she said.

Pushing back her own chair and getting up, Lisa realised she would rather have prayed alone just now, but she stood, obediently, and said the words of praise with Barbara, and asked forgiveness for her own lie, and received Barbara's blessing.

This time it was a quieter experience, more of a recitation than an emotional release. She felt separate from what she was doing, and when she raised her eyes from the grey carpet and looked at Barbara she didn't see the almost incandescent figure she had seen on the platform, she saw only a woman with clasped hands whose finger ends had a stubby, slightly ragged look, as if perhaps she bit her nails.

Lisa told herself that praying could not always be as happy as it had been at the meeting, sometimes praying would have to be serious, would have to be hard work. That made sense.

When she left she walked down the path slowly, to give her mind a chance to settle. She was planning to take Mother Grundy out as soon as she got home, then her parents wouldn't have time to ask anything, and she wouldn't have to unravel the lie about where she had been, not just yet.

What she really wanted to do was go to sleep. She felt as though she had been remade, carefully, gently, delicately remade, and then Barbara had abruptly added new things, dark things that didn't at the moment seem to fit comfortably.

She went out through the gate and closed it behind her.

There was a time when she would barely have seen the gate. Now, she noticed the miniature landscape of chipped paint and split wood that was the top bar and the glossy brown beetle that trekked along it, making a great business of climbing up and over the long splinters. She was reassured to see that everything still looked more like itself than ever before.

She walked carefully along the pavement, paying attention to each step, thinking something out. She knew that Flora always saw things like this. The things had not changed, it was her own way of looking at them that had changed, and with it, her way of looking at herself. But it was more than that. Her own appearance had changed in some way, Flora had noticed it, Flora had said so. Lisa had learnt a few months earlier that outward appearances are affected by inner changes, but she had forgotten the lesson until now – and she had never expected it to apply to her.

It had been Lisa, returning some freshly washed marmalade pots, who had found Mrs Paxton dead.

She had hurried in through the front door, which had never been locked, calling a greeting, the clean pots still hot from the sterilizing scalding her mother had given them.

She had found Mrs Paxton in the sitting room, in front of the television, sitting comfortably in her chair, her head drooping down towards her shoulder, like a plump bird with its head under its wing.

There had been other times when Mrs Paxton had slept through her arrival, but had woken easily enough to a gentle shake. That final time, though, Lisa had made no attempt to do anything but put down the jam jars, switch off the TV, and back away towards the door. Although she had never seen anyone dead before she had known, instantly, the difference between a sleeping figure and one that was empty of life. When she had run to fetch her mother she had heard herself say, "Mrs Paxton's gone," because that had seemed to be an exact account of what had happened.

Now, as she reached her own gate, unlatched it and went in, she wondered why she had begun to think of death.

· CHAPTER FIFTEEN ·

IN SPITE OF, or more probably because of, the immensity of what had happened to her, Lisa still hadn't said anything to her parents two weeks later.

Flora, who could picture their reaction, understood completely, and said nothing to Katherine either, in case she should feel bound to pass the word across the fence.

Barbara retained her conviction that Lisa would know when the time had come.

No one – not Flora and, more surprisingly, neither Barbara nor anyone else in the group – thought to ask her how she managed the secrecy, despite the fact that she went on both Sundays to the service at Ellesdon Court Hotel, and also called in often at the house to join Barbara's study and prayer sessions.

The answer was that she continued to lie. If Flora chanced to be off out somewhere at the relevant time, Lisa would tell her parents that she was going too. If not, she would say she was visiting Carrie or staying on at school to do her homework in the library. She never involved anyone else in her lies – neither Flora nor Carrie even knew about them – and she took minimum precautions when she was going to the house. She chose to see the fact that her parents remained in complete ignorance of her activities, against all the odds, as a sign that the lies were not sins.

She knew that throughout history people had kept their

faith secret in the face of all kinds of threats and dangers, and it seemed to her insulting to their memory, as well as faintly ridiculous, that she should do the same just because she thought her parents might tease her. Yet somehow she couldn't find a way to raise the subject with them.

She apologised for this, on her knees, alone in her room.

She brought anxiety to each session of prayer. She didn't know what to say, she didn't know how to ask forgiveness for the secrecy and the lies when she was unable to promise to stop them – and she was afraid she might really be as deluded as her parents would think her, if they knew. But by the end of each short hesitant prayer, all anxiety had been lifted from her and she felt completely happy and extraordinarily safe.

Each time she began, she was afraid that she would fail to make contact with the power and the glory she had glimpsed at that first meeting, and each time it was there, waiting for her. She knew, although Barbara never told her this, that she was only connecting with the very edge of something, the hem, a fingertip, but she knew, also, that that was as much as she needed, as much as she could stand – and that there was a great wall of benevolence that would never let her get too close to the fire.

She and Goldie still walked through bandit-country in the afternoons, but now they had to go directly after school because darkness came earlier and earlier.

Usually there was someone working on one or other of the allotments, harvesting late vegetables, or tidying up amongst dry snapping stems, or hanging up bulbs to over-winter. Lisa supposed there always had been people there, she just hadn't noticed them before. When there was some-body in one of the three plots nearest the fence, she took to calling out a greeting as she passed. She was surprised to find they knew her by sight, and that the stout woman who grew the dahlias even knew Goldie by name, her true name, not her Mother Grundy name.

She began to admire the tip, a very superior one which was not open to garbage trucks but only accepted bottles, newspapers, broken fridges, builders' rubble and other non-smelly rejects, which were neatly grouped, like with like for recycling.

She noticed that crows were not the only birds in the cemetery trees, there were other, smaller ones, all different. Some, like the robin and the blue tits, she could even name.

The fence dispute began to seem totally irrelevant to her. It had reached an impasse, with Katherine insisting the base of the new one must be put where the base of the old one had stood, not where its top had rested when it fell, and Barbara continuing to say that the trench was correctly placed according to the deeds of Mrs Paxton's house.

"Land is land," Lisa said to Flora. "It's part of the earth, what does it matter where a fence stands?"

Flora, who was beginning to feel slightly guilty for being so territorial, didn't argue.

At school Lisa was more outgoing, and one or two new friendships began to seem possible. Flora's birthday party, early in November, was the first party she had ever attended with enthusiasm.

Her parents did, eventually, notice a change in her, as Barbara had predicted. However, they didn't make much of it. Her father just said, "Nice to see you a bit more cheerful these days."

"As cheerful as the Hallelujah Hall lot?" said Lisa, casually, thinking this was a useful opening.

It turned out not to have been an opening after all.

"All that grinning and singing doesn't necessarily mean anything," said her father.

"I suppose," said Lisa, even more casually, not looking at either of them, "that all religious communities must think they've got something the rest of us haven't."

"Possibly," said her mother, "but that sort of thing isn't for people like us."

Lisa knew what she meant by 'people like us', she meant normal people.

"I sometimes wonder if all that singing isn't a bit like yoga breathing exercises," her mother went on. "If you deprive yourself of oxygen, you're bound to think you see visions."

"*You* go to church, though," said Lisa, "occasionally."

"Oh well, you can come along to church sometimes, if you want to," said her mother, looking at her rather attentively for the first time since the conversation had begun. "But just don't go letting it take over your life, the way they have, it isn't healthy."

"Old women and teenage girls," said Lisa's father, giving her a brief hug which she pulled away from, "often go through a religious phase." He smacked his forehead, grinned, and said, "Trust me to have a daughter who wants to become a nun."

Lisa thought of what Barbara had said about nuns, with their idolatrous crucifixes and their devotion to the Virgin Mary, who had been human and therefore should never be the focus of prayers. She wondered briefly if it would help if she told her father that Barbara's views on nuns were similar to his own, then decided that even if they had the same attitudes, they held them for different reasons, and it was all too complicated for her. She let the subject drop, and, with some relief, so did they.

She didn't feel able to talk about any of this to Barbara, either, or at least not unless Barbara somehow introduced the subject first. But Barbara never did.

Although the big meetings still had almost the same effect on her as the first one, she found the smaller sessions in the house left her ruffled and slightly disconnected. She accepted this without question. She could see that the one area was about love and the other was about learning, and learning was bound to be more effort.

It was at the house sessions that Barbara explained about

103

the traps and snares that were laid by Satan. "The more you declare for Jesus," she said, "the more danger you are in, because you have issued a challenge to Satan, and make no mistake, he will take up that challenge. You are caught up in a war, the mightiest and most important war that has ever taken place, or ever will take place, on this earth."

She explained what was wrong with astrology. "It's an affront to Jesus," she said, "and anything that is offensive to Jesus comes from Satan. It is not given to us to know the future and we shouldn't try to do so. Our faith is all we need, we don't need the imaginary help of planets."

She taught that talismans and amulets were pagan devices, which should be thrown away, if currently owned, and avoided in future. "Magic is blasphemy," she said. "If a miracle is to be wrought it will be wrought by Jesus, not by some heathen god or nature spirit."

She also broke the news to Lisa that it was a mistake to keep pets. She didn't suggest getting rid of Goldie, but she did point out that all love should be directed towards God and not squandered on domestic animals. "Remember," she said, "that the world is in Satan's power, so his magical devices are everywhere, waiting to trap us. And the more innocent they look, the more dangerous they are, because the more likely we are to be deceived by them."

Lisa listened carefully, grateful for the warnings, but sometimes when she got home her mind was so full of Satan and his dangers that she found it hard to concentrate on anything else.

With her new awareness of bandit-country, she noticed that there seemed to be more carrion crows than before, and definitely more foxes, who were quite often boldly visible in the daytime and who left the mangled remains of pigeons and, once, a rat scattered about. She had to pull hard on Goldie's collar to keep her questing jaws away from them.

She was stern with herself about not wanting to believe in Satan. She thought she was being childish only to want the magnificent, generous part and not the vicious, negative part.

She was uncertain whether Satan existed as a being, or as an evil force. What she was certain of was that he must be watching, all the time, the way the commander of an opposing army would watch. She wondered if he saw through physical eyes, or in some other way. If through physical eyes, then surely he would use the carrion crows, the foxes, the rats, the dark order of things that lived on the edge, touching on human habitation, and sometimes dipping into it.

The bright colours and late flowers which had flourished in October were slowly but relentlessly subdued by the dark and damp of November. The clear cold sunny air was deadened by low cloud and contaminated with drifting vapours. Conkers lost their glossy, confident look and began to dry out and shrink. The fat, sweet blackberries on the bushes at the edges of the allotments had all been picked and enjoyed, and their successors were small and unpleasant-looking. The bright leaves, that had hung like celebratory pennants from the Sumak tree on the corner of the road, lay on the pavement, and became as slimy and malicious as all the other fallen leaves, making shoes slip and push-chairs and wheeled shopping-baskets skid sideways.

In many ways, Lisa was experiencing her first winter. She had lived through the ones that had gone before without allowing them to touch her, and now she was inclined to be dismayed by the smell of decay and the sight of so many things apparently coming to an end.

Flora was reassuring. "It's all right," she said cheerfully. "The year's going into the dark, and then in the spring it will come out into the light again. There's nothing bad about that."

"But we're supposed to love everything that God made," said Lisa, "and I don't like this at all."

She mumbled, rather, because she was still a little embarrassed, talking about God. She would probably have felt easier if she could have found some other name for the enormity that had so recently discovered her, but it didn't occur to her to try.

Flora had no such problems. "It's all a pattern," she said. "The year dies and lies quiet and then wakes up again. The corn god is beheaded, and ground up for bread, and then a few ears are put in the earth and he rises again. Jesus is crucified, dead and buried, and then resurrected."

"You say you're not a Christian," said Lisa, "but then you talk as though you are."

"Like I say," said Flora, "it's a pattern. Things only seem to be dead. It's a stage they have to go through."

"But do you believe the pattern is made by God?"

"I don't know about names," said Flora. "But I believe in something. People have known about it forever – even the stone-agers had their sacred places."

"That's not the same thing," said Lisa. "It isn't what I mean."

"It might be the same," said Flora simply. "They didn't have the chance to be Christians, if that's what you mean, but they may have got it as nearly right as anybody else."

"They could have been Devil-worshippers and Satanists," said Lisa, wondering why she was discussing the ancient past when she needed to talk about the present.

"We'll never know," said Flora.

· CHAPTER SIXTEEN ·

IT WAS SOME while before Lisa would admit to herself that her friendship with Flora was changing.

Gradually, she found she felt subtly threatened by the Scorpio charm and the silver Ankh which gleamed at her from around Flora's neck. She was unexpectedly uneasy in the presence of Jack's new interest in vampire bats and his hopes of keeping one as a pet, and for some reason she still felt uneasy even when Katherine said he couldn't. Katherine's big untidy back room, with Tabitha sleeping on a pile of astrology books and the corner shelf stacked with herbal medicines, the bottles glimmering in the evening candlelight, began to look more and more like a witch's kitchen. The fact that Barbara suggested that she shouldn't visit too often didn't help.

She didn't want to believe there was evil in the house, and yet its occupants seemed to have enmeshed themselves in an elaborate spider's web of magical and mysterious things. If these things really were attractive to demonic forces, if their use really could open the mind to malevolent influences, then Flora was, at the very least, at risk. Worse than that, she might already be partly won over, perhaps even without knowing it. On one level she still felt the same about Flora as she always had. On another she was afraid for her; and sometimes almost – though never quite – afraid of her.

These thoughts kept coming back and back at Lisa; even when she believed her mind was fully occupied they would find a way in. They hit her with a physical impact, making her stomach shiver and her knees weaken. She could not, would not, make herself believe anything really bad about Flora – and yet she couldn't be sure she was fit to judge. Barbara had emphasised again and again that Satan was shrewd and cunning and well able to make his servants and devices seem appealing. Flora's words kept echoing in her memory: "The world's going into the dark," she'd said, "there's nothing bad about that." It was true that Flora had been talking about the seasons, that she had talked about spring and resurrection as well, but was it the dark that really pleased her, Flora with her annual Hallowe'en party?

Each time Lisa left Hallelujah Hall, Barbara would say, "Bring Flora with you soon. Don't pressure her, but keep asking her. It is important, she is in some danger." Lisa would duly issue an invitation, but Flora would always refuse. She refused in the same easy-going way she did everything yet somehow her decision always sounded final, unarguable. "No, it's OK, it's your thing," she'd say. "Tell me about it after, I like to hear."

In truth, Flora was quite relieved that Lisa had discovered an interest of her own. She was genuinely fond of her, but just sometimes she felt a bit more responsible for her free time than she would have liked. She wasn't aware of it when they were together; but if Lisa had opted out of something because other friends were included, then Flora was often distracted from what she was doing by images of her feeling bored, or rejected, or fat. She was surprised but very pleased to see the change that came over her after her unexpected conversion.

Gradually, though, Flora began to notice other changes. It seemed to her that there wasn't one new Lisa, but two. The buoyant one, the one who had come out of her dream into reality, fizzing with energy and excited by the world, was still around, but occasionally she was replaced by a tense, distracted, extraordinarily difficult one. Flora had grown used to Lisa being a bit dejected occasionally, but she had never before met the moods that now came and went so unpredictably – sudden agitation, minutes on end of a silence that seemed so full of sorrow it was painful to see, occasional flashes of apparently unreasonable anger.

If she asked what was the matter, Lisa, who couldn't explain, would snap at her. If she waited, the state would change and Lisa would be euphoric again, talking, laughing, easy to be with.

Lisa was well aware of her own behaviour, and though she didn't like the unevenness of it, she thought it would pass, in time, and that she would become like everyone else in the group, calm and smiling. She knew Flora was being patient, and she was grateful. But even Flora's patience had its limits.

They had gone shopping together, on a dreary November Saturday. Lisa had been frowning and silent in the record shop and no better in the card shop or around the little cluster of market stalls on the empty plot beside the green-grocer's. Flora stopped pretending she didn't notice and hustled her into the Health Shop. "I can't stand you like this," she said simply, "I'm going to buy you a present! I'm going to aromatherapise you!"

Katherine had all the aromatherapy products at the front of the shop, near the till. When they went in, though, she was deep in conversation with a customer who wanted to understand more about Celestial Tea than it said on the packet, and there were three more people waiting behind him, so Flora decided to make her choice without advice.

"You need something to relax you," she said. "It works wonders with Grandma."

"Oh, I don't know . . ." said Lisa, doubtfully.

"It's all right, I'm not going to start massaging you with perfumed oils. They're too expensive anyway. Now, what do we need?" She picked up one of the leaflets from the side of the rack and began flicking through it.

Lisa had been coping with successive waves of peculiar feelings all morning. Most had been brought on by the sight of yet another example of one of the dangers Barbara had warned her against. The rest had been triggered by things she couldn't judge, things Barbara hadn't specifically mentioned. Now, seeing Flora running her fingers lightly along a line of scented candles, and hearing her say, "I'm going to buy you one of these. Just give me a minute to work out which smell you need," she felt the familiar feeling, a mixture of numbness and jangling, come over her yet again.

"No, Flora, don't," she said. "Not until I ask Barbara."

Flora looked at her in total amazement. "What do you mean, ask Barbara?" she said.

"Well, I have to ask her if it's all right," said Lisa. She lowered her voice. "Some of these things are bad," she muttered. Her mouth seemed to be drying up. Her tongue kept sticking to it, so that it was hard to speak. She couldn't look at Flora, not only because she could sense that Flora was staring at her as if she had just arrived from an alien planet, but because she was horribly aware of how many of the things Barbara had marked out as evil were scattered casually around Flora's house.

She turned quickly and pushed her way through the browsing customers and onto the street. It was the first time she had ever walked out on Flora.

Flora followed.

"Are you telling me," she said, on the pavement, beside the plate-glass window with its display of water filters, "that you have to ask Barbara's permission before I can buy you a scented candle!"

"Some things have other meanings," said Lisa, "that we don't know about."

Then she did look at Flora and saw, not hostility as she had somehow imagined, but sympathy and surprise.

"Anything to do with magic," she said, in a stronger voice, "is bad, it's from Satan. That's why Ed was so against using the Rescue Remedy that first day. Don't you remember?"

"I would *not* buy you a Satanic candle, Lisa," said Flora. "I absolutely guarantee and promise you that I would *not!*" She started to giggle. "Do you really think Mum's going to sell black magic stuff in the *Health* Shop," she said, "and let Grandma be anointed with demonic oils!"

Lisa laughed grudgingly. "I just meant I'm not sure," she said, "that's all. Be fair – all this is new to me."

"Yes, and I don't know if it's doing you much good," said Flora.

"It's the only thing in the world that really matters," said Lisa. "It *is* the world. If you'd just come to one of the meetings you'd understand."

"I tell you what I *don't* understand," said Flora. "I don't understand what went wrong. At the beginning you were kind of . . . I don't know – lit up, almost. You were happy. But now you've gone all peculiar and sort of twitchy."

"Only sometimes," said Lisa reasonably. "Mostly I feel great."

"Yes, but the sometimes's are happening more often," said Flora. "You can stop going in there any time you want, you know."

"Never!" said Lisa. "That isn't it; I know what it is. I've got to sort things out in my mind. I'm just a bit slow."

"You're not slow and you're not fat," said Flora automatically. "What is it, really? You can tell me, I won't send you up."

"All right," said Lisa, already overburdened with secrecy, "I'll tell you. It's that if you let God into your mind, you have to let Satan in, too, and it's scary."

"No!" said Flora. "No, never, that *can't* be right!"

"I have to," said Lisa, "because I have to be aware of him so that I can keep free of him. It's perfectly logical."

111

"I think you've got very confused somewhere along the line," said Flora, and she caught hold of Lisa's sleeve and led her away from the window. "And I think we should check it out *urgently*."

Lisa was too concerned with her own inner anxieties to notice which way Flora was pulling her, or to remember what stood next to the Health Shop. She was already walking through the heavy door Flora was holding for her, her mind working on how best to explain Barbara's teaching, when she saw where they were.

They were walking into the bank and Flora was saying, "We'll ask Ed, and whatever he says I'll go along with."

"No," hissed Lisa, hanging back. "Flora, didn't you know? Ed's gone . . ."

But Ed had not gone from the bank, he was in his usual place behind the Foreign Exchange till, and he had no customers. He saw them at once and Flora, who hadn't been listening to Lisa's urgent hissing, walked right up to him. Lisa, her face red as much with confusion as embarrassment, followed her.

· CHAPTER SEVENTEEN ·

I T WAS THE peculiar interview with Ed that finally persuaded Flora into Hallelujah Hall.

She was aware that it was not entirely fair to corner someone at work and expect him to pronounce on matters of faith across the counter. All the same she had been quite sure that she knew what he would say, and also how he would say it: reassuringly, smilingly, confidently. With Lisa, flustered, hovering behind her, she smiled through the shatter-proof glass and began to explain their problem.

Ed, though, was visibly thrown. Since no one seemed in immediate need of foreign currency, he was able to come out from behind his counter and shepherd them gently over to a position near the door. There he stood, between an artificial Weeping Fig and a rack of leaflets about Pension Schemes, looking anxious.

"I just want you to tell Lisa that she doesn't have to spend her life dodging Satan," said Flora. "That he isn't hiding in the aromatherapy candles."

Ed sighed. "There *are* dangers," he said, "and they can come from unexpected quarters. I'm not really the person to ask, just at the moment."

Now that she could no longer avoid the confrontation, Lisa found she didn't feel embarrassed any more.

"Ed's left," she said to Flora. "He isn't next door any

113

more. If we need to know anything, we have to ask Barbara."

"Left?" said Flora, to Ed. "Why?"

There was a tiny pause before Ed spoke. Then, "I've joined the Pentecostal Church," he said. "Why not come along?" At last he smiled. "It has music and joy and none of the unnecessary formality of the so-called traditional church. I can let you have details of services . . ."

But Flora was not to be deflected. "What went wrong next door?" she said, and without even knowing what she did, she reached out and put her hand protectively on Lisa's arm.

Ed watched her for a moment, but it was obvious he was not really seeing her, his attention was all inward. Then, "If there's a falling-out between people," he said, "it isn't easy for either side to discuss it without insulting the other. I don't want to dishonour fellow Christians."

"Come on," said Lisa, pulling her arm away from Flora's hand. "He doesn't want to talk to us. Let's go."

Flora, though, stood her ground. "Is there some reason," she said, "why Lisa shouldn't go next door?"

"Lisa found God through the Group," said Ed, "that's what matters." He paused, started to speak, stopped and then began again. "Just remember," he said, "that Lucifer himself was once an angel. Even the highest angel can fall."

Flora stared at him a moment longer, and then shrugged and allowed Lisa to pull her away.

"Let's meet in a week or so," said Ed, raising his voice as they drew away from him, "and talk again, when I've got my head together."

But they were out of the door before he had finished speaking.

They argued most of the way home, a quiet, intense argument with long pauses. When they reached Cemetery Road neither had any memory of the journey, though each had sharp recollections of the hostile profile of the other.

114

Flora was sure that Ed had been issuing a coded warning against Barbara and the group. Lisa was equally certain that he had been confessing to his own fall from grace. Flora said that Ed simply wasn't ready to talk yet; they must wait and speak to him again when he was.

Lisa said, "You only want to listen to Ed because you fancy him."

Flora said, "That is *so* unfair. I'm trying to understand something."

They didn't entirely know how they reached the front doorstep of Mrs Paxton's old house, either, and when Lisa angrily rang the bell, and Flora irritably allowed herself to be welcomed inside, they were neither of them in the least prepared for what was to come.

They were welcomed in by Mrs Fisher, the woman who had stood by Lisa at her first big service, and who Lisa had not seen since. She recognised them both and was clearly very happy to see them. "Barbara's conducting a small healing service in there," she said, gesturing towards the front room. "Go on in."

Lisa hesitated and Flora said, "We don't want to interrupt, we'll come back."

"No, my dear," said Mrs Fisher, "it's open to anyone. It'll be followed by a short thanksgiving, and that's such a lovely thing to be part of." She gave Lisa a quick hug. "I'm so glad you've brought your friend," she said. "Take her on in, there's a good girl, you know there's no formality here."

As they walked towards the closed door they could hear voices, one stronger, one weaker, though they couldn't hear what was being said. It was a little like being outside a doctor's surgery when a consultation is taking place. Lisa, confident and sure of her welcome, opened the door and walked in. Flora, conscious of being on foreign soil, tried to hang back – but Lisa held the door for her and she followed.

There were several people in the plain room, their faces familiar but not well known. They looked concerned but calm and they were gathered around Barbara who was talking quietly to a young man, younger than Ed, who was kneeling on the ground with his hands covering his face. "When you're ready," Barbara was saying gently, "whenever you're ready."

She looked up and smiled as Lisa closed the door behind them. "Come in," she said. "Lisa, Flora, come in. Join us in praying for our brother here."

Then the young man began to talk in a low monotone, and the others, some of whom had been murmuring prayers, fell silent, and Barbara reached out and put her hands on the young man's head. In the quietness of the room his words could be heard clearly. He was making a confession, relentlessly, without pauses, as though he felt that if he hesitated he would not be able to go on. It was an extraordinary confession, to do with shoplifting and pornographic magazines and bad dreams, and if she had heard it in any other context Flora might have found it difficult not to laugh. It didn't seem funny, though, in that quiet room, in that quiet drone; it seemed pathetic, and personal, and almost eerie. Flora did not know what she had expected, but nothing like this. Appalled, she turned to Lisa and whispered, "We must go, this is private."

But Lisa shook her head, and in any case two people were somehow between them and the door, people who smiled reassuringly and gestured that it was all right for them to stay.

Suddenly the young man started to weep, giving great gasping discordant sobs, as though he didn't know how to cry properly; and then Barbara was speaking, loudly enough for him to hear her voice above his own noise, telling him that it was all right, that none of it was his fault, that it was Satan acting in him and all he had to do was renounce Satan and he would be free of all such thoughts and acts.

Most of the other people in the room moved towards Barbara, as if to give her support, and some began to sing softly. Then Barbara was giving the young man the words of renunciation, and he was chanting them after her. His voice was as harsh as a crow's, and he seemed out of control of it, so that it rose and fell in a peculiar rhythm.

All at once he was convulsing, down on the floor, and Barbara was on her knees, holding his head, and someone else was there, doing something to his mouth so he couldn't swallow his tongue, and the cries he was making sounded like death, and Flora dug her fingers into Lisa's arm and said, "I have to get out!"

Lisa, who was as frightened as she was, hesitated for a moment, unsure whether the scene was really as nightmarish as it seemed, or if it was only because she was seeing it through Flora's eyes – and in that moment of hesitation everything changed.

The twisted figure on the floor stopped choking and sank back as if he had fallen asleep. Barbara and the man nearest to her lifted him gently into a sitting position, supporting him one on each side, and everyone else began to sing a song of praise that was astonishingly loud and rich for such a small group.

Lisa felt the familiar joy ballooning up in her chest, and tears running down her face. She unhooked Flora's terrified fingers from her arm and held her by both wrists. "See!" she said, almost shouting so Flora would hear above the singing. "It's all right. They've cured him, he's better. You've seen the horrible bit, you have to stay for the lovely bit!"

Within minutes, they had the young man on his feet, white-faced but smiling weakly, and two people led him gently, kindly, slowly out of the room. Each one of those remaining in the room reached out to touch him softly as he passed – all except Lisa, who wanted to, but was holding

Flora, and Flora herself who was now standing rigidly in Lisa's grip, with no expression on her face at all.

The song ended and Barbara moved over to them. Her eyes glittered and two spots of colour burned on her cheeks. "Don't look so worried," she said to Flora, "he's been purged of something dreadful that was driving him to do squalid and negative things. He's free of it. Now he needs to rest, and then he can start his life all over again."

Flora heard the words, and like Lisa she could sense the happiness of the others in the room, but the sight of the young man, apparently held down, apparently pushed to some kind of limit, had shocked her beyond speech.

She looked at Lisa and saw Barbara's unusually bright eyes and pink face reflected there. She turned to go, but Barbara stopped her, without moving or making any attempt at physical restraint, simply by wanting to, simply by knowing she could. "You've been upset by something you don't understand," she said. "Please don't leave until you *do* understand, don't carry away a false impression. We were not harming him. Satan had him in his power, but Satan has been forced to leave him, he has been saved."

Flora's voice returned to her. "I don't understand what you're doing," she said, "but I don't want to be in a room where you're doing things with Satan."

"You are always in a room with Satan," said Barbara, and her voice was ice and fire, "unless you deny him. He lives in you."

"No," said Flora, and she stepped backwards, thinking that she was moving nearer to the door, but she bumped into something hard, and putting her hands behind her she felt the wall. The door was near, but she couldn't turn away from Barbara to look for it.

Lisa let go of Flora's wrists and turned towards Barbara, and one of the other people in the room moved forward and said, "Gently, Barbara, the child's had a fright," but Barbara continued to hold Flora with her eyes, saying, "I can take Satan away from you, Flora. You and I together can push him out of your life forever."

"Satan isn't *in* my life!" said Flora, and her voice was unsteady. "Let me go!"

Lisa found the door, dragged it open and turned to guide Flora through it, but the room seemed to have shrunk and the figures that filled it all seemed to be moving, this way or that, and she couldn't reach her. Her hand touched Mrs Fisher, who bent down to speak in her ear. "It's all right, Lisa," said Mrs Fisher, in a voice distorted by Lisa's own fear. "I think you should both go now. Barbara's very tired, this is all too strong."

"Yes, Flora, Satan *is* in your life," said Barbara, the only person in the shifting room who remained sharply in focus. "He is in all the mysteries you are interested in, he is in the pagan symbols you wear around your neck, he is in your mother's belief in astrology and primitive magic. But there is nothing to be afraid of, only deny him and you will be free . . . freedom is here for you!" And she began to repeat the words she had said for the young man, before he had collapsed, before he had revived.

"I won't say your spells!" shouted Flora, and somehow the shouting made her begin to gag, as though she might be going to be sick.

"See!" said Barbara, in a strong voice, and the shape of the word made her mouth stretch back from her teeth. "The Great Satan doesn't wish to be banished!"

The room became still – people who had seemed to be moving closer to Barbara, as if to restrain her, hesitated, watching her, watching Flora.

Flora stared back, gulping, trying to get control of her throat.

"Just say you no longer accept Satan in your life, my love," said Mrs Fisher, into the silence, putting her arms round Flora. "That's all you have to say and you'll feel better."

Her normal voice, her comforting action, deflected the power of Barbara's focus for a moment, and Flora's voice returned to her with full strength.

"If I say that," she said, with such force that she held the attention of the whole room, "it will mean that I have been accepting your Satan in my life up to now – and I have not – and my mother has not – and we are not evil – and we are not interested in evil – and I don't want to hear about evil – and I don't want to think about evil – and I won't let you make me!"

She pulled herself free of Mrs Fisher, who in any case made no attempt to stop her, and ran out of the room, pushing people aside as she went, and her footsteps echoed across the hall and then the front door slammed.

Lisa, turning to follow, her mind full of the sight of Flora's white, tear-wet face, her legs shaking so much that she hardly knew if they would carry her, felt herself caught and held back.

"Wait," said Barbara, and her voice seemed ordinary and warm again, and she smiled her familiar smile. "She'll be all right. Don't follow her until you're calmer or you'll upset each other."

Lisa, unable to look anywhere but into Barbara's face, was aware of others speaking in the room. Too shaken to concentrate at first, she could only grasp disconnected phrases, but they seemed concerned, upset, unhappy.

"Leave us!" said Barbara, over her shoulder, speaking to the room in general. "If you have doubts we'll talk them over later – this is not the time."

They didn't all go, but those who stayed remained silent while Barbara, her gaze holding Lisa's, said, "Flora will be all right, Lisa. It was not Flora you saw choking and crying, it was the demons in Flora who didn't want to be displaced. But she's made a good start. She used her own words, not mine, but she has denied evil. It's the first essential move. You know that's right, don't you?"

"Yes," whispered Lisa.

"And you want your friend to be saved?"

"Yes," said Lisa, sure of that at least.

"Good," said Barbara. "Now stay and sing with us so that you are calm and happy before you see her again."

At her signal, one of the loveliest of the Gospel songs began to fill the room. Yet somehow it didn't seem as powerful as usual, as though the singers were hesitant, unsure.

Lisa thought it must be her fault. She thought she was not hearing it right because she had doubted Barbara; because she had wanted to run away and take Flora; and because if she had succeeded in taking Flora away, then Flora would not, after all, have the chance to be saved.

· CHAPTER EIGHTEEN ·

LISA WAS WALKING through bandit-country, away from home, towards the world beyond the railway line. She couldn't tell if Goldie was with her or not. Ahead of her there stood a man, with his back to her, a tall man wearing a white robe that came down to his feet. His hair was thick and hung below his shoulders; brown, except where the sun touched gold into it. Even though his back was towards her, she could see that his arms were held out in blessing, and all over the ground in front of him plants were pushing up out of the earth and bursting into flower.

Lisa moved towards him, as fast as she could, hardly knowing if she was running or flying. The man seemed to hear her approach, because he turned towards her. As he faced her, as she reached him, she saw that his hands were not open in blessing, but curved inwards like predatory claws, and his bearded face was malicious, the eyes evil.

Her own scream woke her up, though as she heard its sound dying away she realised it had not been loud, not really a scream at all, rather a gasp of horror.

She had been awake most of the night, but still she sat up in bed and put on the bedside lamp, frightened of going to sleep again. The pulsing red numbers on the clock told her it was nearly five in the morning.

She had not followed Flora. She had stayed for a while in the plain room with the grey carpet, listening as Barbara explained to her how crucial it was that Flora should be separated from her pagan connections.

"Flora isn't evil, but there are evil things in Flora," Barbara had said. "I understand why you don't want to believe that, but you must trust me. I have been called to this ministry and I know things that you can only guess at. You must make sure that Flora comes here again."

Lisa had not been aware she was shaking her head until Barbara had told her to stop.

"Be very careful indeed," Barbara had said. "You have discovered the most wonderful thing there is – but you must share it or lose it. If you are jealous of Flora, however secretly, and if you try to keep this for yourself, you will find that you have shut yourself off from it. God will turn away from you."

Even with that unthinkable possibility in her mind, Lisa could not face Flora straight away. She imagined Flora angry with her, hurt, and throwing out all kinds of arguments that she would not be able to answer. The responsibility seemed too much and she went straight home, had no difficulty in convincing her parents that she wasn't well, and went to bed early.

This was a mistake, though, because it made the night very long. Dreary dark hours inched by as Lisa lay in bed, too tired and confused to think, simply allowing thoughts to move through her mind, some of them desolate, many of them frightening.

With her eyes closed she watched a parade of memories of all the things in Flora's house she had once thought so lovely, and which now she must believe were full of menace.

Later she realised, with a sense of shock, that Barbara had never insisted that she set aside Satan, the way she had directed that Flora must. Yet Satan owned the world and therefore owned her.

She knelt on the floor by the bed and tried to repeat the words of renunciation that Barbara had dictated, but she couldn't remember them properly, wasn't sure if it was working, was in any case reluctant to mention the name of all evil, on her own and in the dark.

Then she had the nightmare.

By the time daylight arrived she knew she had to take some kind of action or else the nightmare would never properly stop.

There was no lying-in on Sundays in Lisa's house. Her parents usually dedicated the day to home improvements and liked to get breakfast over as soon as possible so they could start. The moment it was cleared away, Lisa said she was going next door, to Flora's.

"Are you sure you're well enough?" said her mother. "You still look very white, and dark about the eyes."

"I'm fine," said Lisa.

"You're not going to give Flora any germs, are you?" said her mother. She pressed her hand onto Lisa's forehead, and then pinched her wrist between thumb and forefinger. "You don't seem feverish," she said, "so I suppose it's all right."

For the first time in the two and a half years since she had moved next door to Flora, Lisa was unsure of her welcome. She stepped over the fence and walked slowly into the kitchen where she found Jack, eating chocolate-cereal, and Grandma, holding a tin and scraping out a repulsive mix of tiny grey fish-heads and colourless jelly onto a saucer. Tabitha stalked to and fro at her feet, legs stiffened to make herself as tall as possible, head up, tail straight, purring loudly.

"Where is everyone?" said Lisa.

It didn't occur to either of them to answer her, but then Flora and Katherine came into the kitchen from the other door, the one that opened into the house. Lisa looked at them, wondering what she should say.

Before she could decide, Flora said quickly to Katherine, "You don't need to tell Lisa what happened."

"All right," said Katherine, and she smiled at Lisa, her usual smile, and walked over to the fridge, stepping over Tabitha who was now hunched over the saucer and eating her way intently through the breakfast that gazed hopelessly and stickily back at her. "Would anyone like some orange juice?"

Before she could pick up the carton, the front door bell rang, and she went out of the room again, leaving Jack and Tabitha eating and Grandma sitting on the stool with her hands on her knees, smiling down at the cat.

Flora beckoned Lisa over to the door and led her just outside, into the passage, well away from listeners. "I didn't tell Mum you were there yesterday," she said quietly. "I didn't lie, she just didn't ask."

She seemed cold, formal, and very, very pale.

Not knowing what to say, Lisa stood still and said nothing.

"I'm really sorry," said Flora.

"What?" said Lisa.

"I shouldn't have run out and left you with them," said Flora, her words piling on top of one another. "It was a terrible thing to do, but I was so confused, and then I thought I should come back, but I couldn't make myself, and you'd said I wasn't to tell anyone so I couldn't get Mum. I watched their door and I saw you come out and go home, and you looked OK – but I thought you might never speak to me again."

"I thought you wouldn't speak to me," said Lisa, astonished at how relieved she felt, "for taking you there."

"I took *you*," said Flora, "that time, anyway. I wanted to straighten you out." She began to giggle, rather shakily. "I picked the wrong place, didn't I!"

"But Barbara was trying to help you," said Lisa. "I know

125

it seemed horrible, but she was only trying to heal you. Truly."

Katherine had opened the front door but she had not brought the visitor inside. Their voices began to drift back through the house.

"I didn't give Mum the whole story," said Flora, "but she almost hit the roof anyway – you *have* to tell your parents – and you *mustn't* go in there again."

"Listen," said Lisa, "that's Barbara at the door!"

Flora mimed putting her fingers in her ears. "Lisa, you saw," she said, "you were there, you won't have anything more to do with her, will you?"

"That's not you talking," said Lisa unhappily. "That's Satan talking."

"What *is* it with these people," said Flora. "Why are they so interested in Satan? They're obsessed! They're supposed to be about love and renewal and respect and good things, but all they do is look for evil."

The voices at the front door were growing louder, making their way across the hall, round the corner and along the passage to where Flora and Lisa stood, outside the kitchen door, in the angle of the wall.

"Flora won't tell me exactly what happened," Katherine was saying, "but she was very upset. In future if you have anything to say, will you please talk to me."

Barbara said something in reply, but she was still outside the door and they couldn't hear the words.

"You prey on the weak," Katherine said in answer. "You try to take away their free will and make them dependent on you."

"Of course we seek out the weak and vulnerable," said Barbara, who had clearly moved closer to the step, allowing her voice to travel as far as Katherine's. "They're the ones who need our help and protection. *Especially* your daughter, who you surround with magic and sorcery!"

"I wish I really was a witch!" said Katherine. "Then I could make a binding spell to keep you away from her."

By silent agreement, the two girls moved quietly along the corridor to the point where it opened onto the front hall. They could glimpse Katherine from the back and Barbara not at all. Unless Katherine looked behind her they would not be seen.

"Don't you see," said Katherine, far too caught up in the conversation to look anywhere but at Barbara, "what you're giving to Satan? All imagination, all mystery, all intuition, all ancient wisdom, all creativity – you're saying the best and richest parts of our experience are his, and I think that's blasphemous, utterly blasphemous."

"You're not in a good position to talk about blasphemy," said Barbara, "filling your house with evil things, encouraging children to play at being witches and demons!"

"If there's any evil here it's in you!" said Katherine. "You build and strengthen the image of Satan – which wasn't in any of our minds before you came. You attend to him and think of him all the time. If he really does have power in the world, then you're feeding it!"

"Katherine's calling her evil!" whispered Lisa, pulling Flora back, away from their eavesdropping position.

"Mum's getting carried away because she's upset," said Flora, "but you know she's right about them always going on about the devil, *and* about them taking away your free will! Even about that stupid candle, you couldn't think for yourself, you wanted to check if it was on some list of nasties they've made up. You just blindly follow that woman!"

"No," said Lisa, "we're following Jesus."

"Are you?" said Flora. "Are you sure?"

The nightmare shimmered threateningly at the edge of Lisa's memory. "But if you'd been there," she said, finding it hard to talk because her mouth was out of shape with grief, "on that first day, at that big meeting . . ."

"That was different," said Flora. "That was good. *I* know that! But I don't believe this is. And why did Ed leave? Think about it, at least *think* about it!"

The front door slammed, but Katherine did not come back down the hall.

"Mum won't have her in," said Flora. "They're fighting on the path, now."

"I love Katherine," said Lisa, surprising herself. "How *can* she think Barbara's evil?"

"No one's evil," said Flora. "It's the fight that's evil. Barbara says Satan likes to divide people – well, good on him. If that's what he wants, he's doing a terrific job out there."

Raised voices could be heard, muffled and distorted by passing through the closed door.

"No, on second thoughts," said Flora, "I don't suppose it is Satan out there, that'd be small potatoes to him. He'll be off causing a war somewhere, needling thousands and thousands of people into fighting over some vast bit of land, with cities and towns and villages and all that stuff. And you know what? He'll be telling each side that he's on the *other* side, so each side will think they're fighting the force of evil itself, and that'll make them fight even harder."

The sound of the front door opening again echoed back to them. There were no more voices, just Katherine's approaching footsteps.

"I'm going home," said Lisa, and she pulled open the kitchen door and hurried through towards the garden before Flora could stop her. Jack was kneeling up at the table, reading a comic which was spread across the half-empty cereal bowl, one corner sopping up chocolate-stained milk. Tabitha, her dish greasy but empty, had settled on Grandma's knee, her purr deep and steady. Grandma was stroking her with both hands, first one then the other, in a hypnotic rhythm.

No one took any notice as Lisa hurried past and out into the garden. Back home she sat on the kitchen floor, her arms round Goldie, resting her cheek against the warm, silky, bony head, and tried to forget that Barbara would have thought her blasphemous for turning to a dog for comfort.

· CHAPTER NINETEEN ·

LATER THAT SAME morning, when Lisa's mother set the coffee machine going and called to Katherine across the fence, Lisa had trouble deciding if she wanted to go to her own room, or stay in the kitchen. Barbara had told her some days earlier that she should set aside time to look through her belongings, to make sure that she didn't own anything with pagan symbolic designs on it, and she still had that to do. On the other hand, she rather wanted to find out what Katherine knew.

She felt guilty at her own cowardice in keeping quiet, but something else had happened to her as well. The intensity of Barbara's instruction had somehow begun to collide in her mind with the unimaginable immensity she had glimpsed. It was as though she stood at the edge of an ocean which stretched far beyond the horizon, and someone placed in her hands a perfect receptacle, designed with precision and devotion to exclude all evil, a receptacle that was strong, and fixed in its form, a receptacle whose sides were not capable of stretching in any direction – and had told her that to save her soul she must somehow fit the ocean into it. Faced with her own inability to understand or obey, she could see only one way out. All she could think of to do was to switch herself off again and sink back into her hazy dream-life, no longer really seeing what she was looking at, no longer really thinking about what was passing through her mind.

When Katherine arrived, Lisa didn't make a decision, she simply stayed where she was, which happened to be in the kitchen. She sat silently beside her mother as Katherine described what she knew of Flora's experience the evening before, and her own confrontation with Barbara that morning.

"Should Flora be on her own?" said Valerie, when she had expressed suitable outrage.

"She's all right," said Katherine. "She seems to have it in perspective. I'm the one who's chewing the furniture in rage."

"All the same . . ." said Valerie.

"She's keeping an eye on Jack," said Katherine, "and she knows where I am. She knows she can come over if she wants."

Lisa, sitting at the kitchen table, flicking through a school history book without actually reading any of the words, was aware that they all glanced at her, but no one said anything, no one asked her what she thought.

"So they're not the easy-going, gentle people you tried to tell me they were," said Lisa's mother, pouring coffee into porcelain cups.

"You can't be religious without being a bigot," said Lisa's father complacently.

"Oh no, Harry, that's not fair," said Katherine.

"They all think they're right," said Harry, "all of them. Each religion thinks it's the only one with the right answers and that every one of the others has got it wrong."

"What on earth's that?" said Lisa's mother, getting up to go to the kitchen window.

Outside, all kinds of noises had begun to trespass on the Sunday silence – thudding and scraping sounds, hammering, voices.

Lisa's mother opened the back door for a better view and

131

Tabitha skidded into the kitchen at an angle, like a car cornering on two wheels, her tail nearly as fat as the whole rest of her body. Goldie, who had seen Tabitha over-excited before, raised her head from her paws, blew down her nose, and rested it back again. Everybody else crowded out of the door, arms folded and shoulders hunched against air that was so cold it felt hard against the skin.

Several people were in the garden beyond Katherine's. They were in working clothes, jeans or dungarees and shabby old sweaters, but they were all familiar, all of them either lived in Mrs Paxton's old house or visited regularly. They were working with their usual cheerful vigour, under Barbara's direction, in two groups.

One group was erecting the new fence, a high, smart, wooden construction, along the line of the trench they had marked out at the start. They were only about three feet out from the house, but they were advancing at some speed.

The other group was digging up the new tree, two people using spades at the roots and a third pulling at the thin, young branches to topple it over.

As Katherine stormed into her own garden and ran towards them, shouting, Flora and Jack appeared outside their kitchen door, looking startled. Katherine veered to one side to shoo them back indoors, and Lisa's parents stepped over their fence in a slightly more restrained manner and hurried towards the scene of activity.

"I think there's some dispute about ownership of this strip," called Harry, friendly, reasonable, firm. "Is it possible to hold up operations until it's sorted out." He wasn't really asking a question.

"Sorry," said Barbara, walking over to him, smiling and shaking her head. She wasn't really apologising.

Lisa, standing outside her own back door, saw Katherine running across to the group by the fence, glancing behind her to make sure Flora and Jack had gone in, and heard her own mother say, "Surely you don't have to destroy the tree, surely you can let it grow on your side of the fence?"

"Sorry," said Barbara again, politely, firmly, with finality, and at that moment Katherine reached them and began shouting at Barbara, so angry that it was hard to understand what she said.

"Yes, it is all right," Barbara said in reply, clearly and calmly. "We're doing the Lord's work on the Lord's day."

Lisa's mother took Katherine by the arm and guided her gently away, saying, "Getting upset won't help, and anyway they've killed it now."

Barbara turned her back on them, pointing, indicating that the thin leafless branches of the hazel tree should be cut up.

Harry took Katherine by the other arm and said to her, "Look, if you're right, you can have them for trespass — let's have a look at the deeds of your house."

"I *am* right," said Katherine, and she began to explain again that they were setting up the new fence where the top of the collapsed fence had lain, not where the foot of it had stood.

Harry cut her short, "Find the deeds," he said, "let's do this officially. Even they can't argue with the law."

He went indoors with her, and Valerie crossed back to her own garden and pushed Lisa gently into the kitchen. "It's too cold to stand around out here," she said, "while people argue points of principle."

Lisa went inside and sat down at the kitchen table again. She found she wasn't thinking about points of principle, or about Barbara's reasons or Katherine's distress; she was thinking about a small tree, with thin whippety branches, that might just have begun to spread its roots and feed the stem bulges that held next year's leaves, and that was now no more than a heap of sap-smelling twigs.

Ten minutes later her father came back in through the kitchen door. Katherine was not with him.

133

"That bit of land *does* belong to Hallelujah Hall," he said. "Katherine's a bit choked about it." He went over to the coffee-maker to refill his cup. "Sometime in the past," he said, "the people who had the house before Katherine must have pinched the land from Mrs P, and she never noticed. I expect they simply made a mistake."

No one noticed that Lisa was quiet during lunch, because neither of her parents felt like saying much either. When she got up at the end, saying she was going over to Carrie's, no one argued, though her mother took her pulse again and asked if she was sure she felt better.

"Yes," said Lisa.

"Must have been a virus," said her mother. "Don't be late back."

The Cadillac had already gone by the time Lisa left the house, but despite the two bus rides, the meeting had not started when she arrived at Ellesdon Court Hotel.

Several people greeted her, including one or two she knew must have been in the morning working party. The meeting didn't seem as crowded as it had before, but whether that was because more of the faces were familiar to her, or because there really were fewer people present, she couldn't be sure.

As she allowed herself to be shunted into the ballroom with the rest, she saw Barbara near the three steps that led up to the platform, talking to Mrs Fisher and two of the men. The conversation seemed to Lisa to be very intense. Because her mind was still full of the morning's conflict – the encroaching fence, the defeated tree – she assumed that was what they must be discussing. Anxious to understand their actions, she sidled between people until she was right beside Mrs Fisher.

Mrs Fisher, seeing her, smiled and said, "Go and find a seat, my love, and I'll come and join you."

The words and voice were gentle, but there was a command in them, and Lisa found herself turning obediently away. As she went she overheard two half-sentences. One of the men said to Barbara, "I'd like to hear more of the words of the Gospels and less *I, I, I . . .*" but the other snapped at him, "You should be careful – you sound like Ed!"

Disturbed, Lisa made her way to the back of the hall, so far back that Mrs Fisher couldn't find her and sat eventually somewhere in the middle, glancing round from time to time in search of her.

Then the singing began, and the power of the meeting filled the room, and Lisa, though she tried to hang onto her anxieties, felt them simply taken from her. The confusion was washed out of her, and with it went the fears and the dark thoughts. By the end she felt she knew for sure what she had always known, that there was nothing evil in Katherine, or in Flora, and that Barbara had misjudged them, misunderstood them in some way. What was more, she was relieved to discover that she knew what she must do next: go home and explain to her parents what the meetings meant to her, whatever they might say about it.

Then Barbara was at her side, saying, "I'll give you a lift home, Lisa."

Lisa thought there were too many people standing around the Cadillac for her to fit in as well, but Barbara guided her to a little Fiat and said, "We'll go in my car."

"I was so happy that you were here today," said Barbara, as Lisa struggled with her seat belt. "I do understand, you know, that old loyalties must be tearing at you."

"Everyone's unhappy," said Lisa, "it's horrible."

"It's a stage," said Barbara, "that has to be gone through. But I knew you would come back, even if not today. I saw you after your first meeting – I knew what had happened to you! I give thanks for you every day, that I was privileged to be part of that!"

Lisa glanced sideways at her as the car pulled out of the

forecourt, and saw the calm, smiling face, the confidence, the certainty that was in her. She remembered Barbara on the platform that first time, her words, the vision she'd shared, the energy she'd poured out into the room. She wondered how she could ever have doubted the judgement of such a person.

"We have exciting news," Barbara went on. "We've bought Ellesdon Court!"

"The whole hotel?"

"Yes, isn't it wonderful! We've been negotiating for some time and everything was confirmed on Friday. I would have told you before, but . . ." She hesitated, then said, "Certain things got in the way." She brightened again. "We can move in very soon indeed and develop it as a centre for the Group."

"You'll move out of the house?" said Lisa, amazed. Another thought intruded. "Why did you do the fence, if you're going anyway?"

"Because the house and garden is our responsibility," said Barbara, "and it's our duty to cleanse it. There is now one more tiny patch of the world that's pure, and safe."

Lisa thought of the empty, cleared garden, the bare, plain house.

"It was a shame about the tree, though," she said. "It was special. It was a memorial to Mrs Paxton, who used to live there."

"Yes," said Barbara, "I gathered that. There's something else I have to tell you. I don't want to dwell on it, but it's important that you know. Lisa, I think that tree said more about Mrs Paxton than it was meant to. It was a hazel tree, a witch's tree."

"Oh no!" said Lisa, startled into vehement response. "It was a hazel because her *name* was Hazel."

"Well," said Barbara, and drove on in silence, leaving the word hanging for a moment or two before she went on. "We found things in the house, things that were left behind after Mrs Paxton's son cleared it. And then, as we expected, we found things under the tree – bad things, awful things."

"There can't have been," said Lisa, and all the uncomfortable thoughts that had dispersed like mist came back, rigid and spiky, and settled in her brain like burrs.

"The hazel tree, the witch tree, was planted with unholy rites," said Barbara. "Extremely unpleasant things had been placed under its roots. I know this will upset you, because you're fond of Katherine and Flora, but I'm afraid it's worse than I thought. I thought they were misguided, but this has to have been deliberate."

"But there were *no* rites," said Lisa. "All we did was we recited a memory we had, of Mrs Paxton, as we planted it. There can't have been any harm in that. And we didn't put *anything* under it."

Barbara was silent.

"But I *know*," said Lisa. "I was *there*!"

"You may have been there when the tree was planted," said Barbara, "but were you there when the hole was dug?"

Lisa began to say that she was . . . and then she remembered. "Well, no," she said, "but they *wouldn't* have."

"The things were there," said Barbara, with finality.

"But what were they?" said Lisa.

"I think it's best not discussed," said Barbara.

"What was in the house?"

"Pagan things," said Barbara. "Innocent enough at first glance, unlike the offerings in the garden. Oriental rugs. But they have symbolic patterns on them, you see, patterns used as an aid in meditation. They are aspects of the Hindu religion and as such they are an offence in the face of God."

Lisa sat stiffly in the passenger seat, pressing her hands together until her nails made little red half-moons on her skin. I have to choose, she thought, between God and everything that is in the world. And she knew she couldn't bear to turn away from the love and the glory that she had glimpsed.

137

"All other religions," she said dully, remembering what her father had said, "they're all wrong?"

"There is only one faith," said Barbara.

"What will happen," said Lisa, "to people who follow other religions?"

"There is only one true God and only one right path," said Barbara. "Those who choose not to follow it are walking towards an eternity that is more terrible than the worst that our minds could ever imagine."

"But good people?" said Lisa. "Devout people? Priests and saints of other religions?"

"I weep for them," said Barbara.

She turned the car into Cemetery Road and pulled up outside Lisa's house.

"You must stay right away from Katherine and that whole family," she said, "right away from them. You can come in to us any time, and later, when we're no longer next door, you can come to the hotel."

"Yes," said Lisa, flatly.

· CHAPTER TWENTY ·

WHEN FLORA OPENED the door of Lisa's room, twenty minutes later, Lisa neither greeted her nor even glanced at her. In any case she had her back to the door. As Flora moved further into the room, she could see that Lisa was crouching down, packing the holdall she used for holidays.

"I saw you come in," said Flora.

Lisa ignored her.

"What are you doing?" said Flora. "Where are you going?"

"They're moving," said Lisa. She didn't need to say who.

"Good," said Flora.

"And I'm going to go and live with them," said Lisa.

There was a short silence. Then, "Do your parents know?" said Flora.

"No."

"You have to tell them. Do you mean you're just going to walk out of here? They'll be off their heads with worry."

"I'm not going tonight," said Lisa, dragging open a drawer and staring at what was inside it. "They're not moving out right away. But I want to be ready to go whenever they say I can."

"How can you want to be with them all the time!" said Flora. "The more you see of them, the more muddled and

139

weird you get. How can that be good? *And* they destroyed the tree!"

"I'm not listening to you," said Lisa, pulling a sweater out of the drawer and folding it with extraordinary care.

"Oh no, of course," said Flora, "I keep forgetting. I'm Satan in disguise, aren't I? Do you *really* believe all that? Do *you* believe it?"

"I believe in possession," said Lisa, still not looking up. She shook the sweater out of its folds and began again. "I can't get myself free if I listen to you and your magic. It isn't your fault, but I can't sort you out, Barbara'll have to see to it."

"How can you be like this?" said Flora. "You make me want to *kick* you. And how can your parents be so stupid – why don't they notice the state you're in?"

"They'd notice if I was a kitchen cabinet," said Lisa sharply. "They'd fix me, or replace me."

"Listen," said Flora, all anger suddenly gone, "they have to know about this. If you can't tell them, I will."

"No!" said Lisa, and now she did turn round and fix Flora with fierce eyes. "You promised!"

"You could release me from the promise."

"I won't release you! Go away – it isn't your business."

"I can't *stand* being the only one who knows," said Flora. "I think they're going to send you off your head . . . You have to talk to someone. Will you talk to someone at school?"

She watched as Lisa unfolded the sweater for the second time and began to fold it in a new way, slowly, meticulously, obsessively. She ran a parade through her mind of every adult she could think of, and stopped at the last one, one she hardly knew, a remote, grey figure who only came to school to teach the senior class, and to do his bit on the platform at assembly on the last day of term. "The vicar," she said. "What's his name, Mr Foster?"

Lisa gave a tight little smile. "Barbara says St Mary's is pagan," she said. "As pagan as you, probably."

Flora turned and walked out of the room. She slammed the door behind her as hard as she could, hoping Lisa's parents would ask why, ran noisily down the stairs and crashed out of the front door.

Lisa's parents, though, were sanding down some shelves in the garden, and the bangs did not sound unusually loud out there.

It was the first time Flora had ever approached St Mary's Church. She had no idea what to expect at five o'clock on a Sunday afternoon – from a congregation to a locked door.

The church seen at a glance, as part of the street, looked tiny, oppressed by the solid height of the block of flats next to it. Looked at on its own, though, it seemed quite a reasonable size, and likely to outlast its thin-walled neighbour. The mesh door at the dark porch entrance, hung there to keep birds out, was unlatched. The wooden church door itself looked more forbidding, but the iron ring turned easily and the door swung inwards on oiled hinges. Flora stepped inside and closed it quietly behind her.

The building seemed empty, though a tiny light burned near the altar with its plain gold cross and two tall candlesticks. It was very quiet. A thin, dry smell of stone rose from the floor, and met the moist scent of old wood. Flora moved cautiously forward and stood behind the last pew, gripping its back in both hands as she looked about her.

A few lights were lit, but shadows were all around and the colours in the stained glass windows above the altar were dim. The flower arrangement opposite the pulpit was made of dahlias, their narrow petals, folded at the base, like a thousand listening ears.

Aware of being a trespasser, Flora stood quietly, waiting to sense rejection, tasting the shadows to see if they were hostile. Deciding they were not, she began look further, up

141

at the roof, like an upturned wooden boat, across at the stone font, around the walls at the memorial tablets.

Then something unexpected caught her eye, at the back of the church, below the organ, and she tiptoed over to it. It was a great, worm-eaten circle of wood with a face carved into it, a face formed of leaves, the stems growing out of the outer corners of the mouth; the Green Man, the pagan woodland god.

A sound made her turn. A door to the left of the altar had opened, and a tall old man with thin grey hair began to walk down the church towards her. Recognising Mr Foster, Flora stood her ground.

"Hallo," said Mr Foster, as he reached her. He nodded towards the ancient leafy head. "That was a roof boss," he said. "When the old rotten roof was taken away, nearly a hundred years ago now, it was all that could be saved."

"It's a nature spirit, isn't it?" said Flora.

"That's right," said Mr Foster. "A powerful pagan symbol." He reached out and touched the head lightly. "We've welcomed him into the sight of God," he said, "and sanctified him." He moved back a little and leant against the nearest pew. "I was just going to lock up," he said, "but I'll wait awhile if you want to have a look round. I should know you from school, shouldn't I?"

Flora told him who she was.

"Of course," said Mr Foster, nodding. "Your mother runs the Health Shop and is very effective at PTA meetings."

Flora smiled. "I wanted to talk to you," she said.

"Well, here you have me," said Mr Foster. "Or would you prefer to come back to the vicarage and drink tea in the study?"

"I'll lose the thread if I have to wait," said Flora. "It's hard to explain."

"Something's worrying you?" said Mr Foster gently.

"My friend has a problem."

"Ah," said Mr Foster.

"No, really," said Flora. "I'm not pretending; it *is* my friend. Except I suppose I do have a problem, and she's it. I thought you might be the right person to talk to about it because you know all about God."

"If I thought I knew all about God," said Mr Foster lightly, "I would be guilty of spiritual pride. Tell me about your friend."

"She's Lisa," said Flora, deciding to throw everything at him at once, so there could be no going back, "and she's started going to Hallelujah Hall – except, I'm sorry, that isn't its real name, it's just what Lisa's father called it, but her parents don't know about her going there – and Barbara, I think she's the minister, she's telling Lisa that Satan is everywhere, she even says this church is pagan, and I think Lisa may think she's possessed, and I know she thinks me and Mum are evil influences, and I probably shouldn't even be in here, because I'm not a Christian – but I really don't know what to do."

Mr Foster didn't say anything straight away, and in the silence Flora slid a little away from him, still gripping the pew-back. When he did speak, though, she realised he had simply been waiting quietly to be sure that she had finished.

"I know about the group you mean," he said. "Next-door neighbours of yours, I think. There are good people there, though some of the things they say are a little saddening."

He inched round the pew's end and sat down, gesturing for Flora to sit, too. She sat at the end of the pew across the aisle from him, sideways so she could face him, though he was gazing towards the altar window, with a dreamy expression.

He looked round at her again. "The idea that the established church is not truly Christian is not new at all, you know," he said. "Like the exaggerated threat of hell-fire, it burns up and dies down to its own rhythm. And we're none of us perfect, of course; humanity isn't."

"They're moving out," said Flora. "I don't know where –
and Lisa says they're taking her with them. So it's urgent!"

The huge, leafy wooden head behind them reminded her,
suddenly, of Lisa looking out of the window at the sycamore, and seeing it for the first time. "I thought it was great
at the beginning," she said, "because after she went there,
she was so *alive* – and I thought, whatever she's got, we
should all get it. Anything that changes someone in that
way has to be good. But she isn't like that any more – she's
gone blank and she's looking for evil everywhere . . . And
if they take her away . . ."

"No, no," said Mr Foster, "they won't take her away. I
think I know where they'll be. They're not going far.
They're buying Ellesdon Court Hotel. I think there may
have been a misunderstanding. I think they probably meant
Lisa could continue to attend services up there, rather than
actually move in. She is a minor and I'm sure they wouldn't
kidnap her, which is what it would amount to." He watched
Flora for a moment. "Have you been to a service?" he said.

"I went into the house," said Flora. "They said I had to
put Satan out of my life. But I can't because he isn't *in* it."

Mr Foster nodded.

"It's scary," said Flora.

"Nothing for you to be scared about," said Mr Foster.
"Something very special seems to have happened to Lisa –
and then to have got a bit confused somewhere. Nothing
that can't be straightened out."

Flora felt a peculiar mixture of relief and guilt; relief at
seemingly having handed the problem over to someone else,
and guilt at what Lisa might think was a betrayal. She also
had a selfish concern that needed to be dealt with.

"You don't think," she said, " – Mum and me – you
don't think we might be . . . sort of . . . in the power of
something?" Abruptly she undid the chain around her neck
and held out the silver Scorpio charm to him. "Because of
things like this," she said.

Mr Foster leant forward and took the charm. He laid it on his palm and looked at it, then leant forward again and handed it back. "Very delicate workmanship," he said. "Flora, there *is* such a thing as demonic possession, but it's extraordinarily rare. What we're talking about here is a kind of spiritual hypochondria. It's just as horrid for the person suffering from it as physical hypochondria. But it can be cured. I'm glad you came to me – we must talk to Lisa. She seems to be giving herself a very nasty time."

"She won't listen to anything against Barbara," said Flora.

"I wouldn't ask her to," said Mr Foster. "Now, how shall we proceed? Could you bring her to see me?"

"She wouldn't come," said Flora.

"Then should I call at the house and speak to her parents, do you think? I know her mother very slightly – she does come to service occasionally."

"That would really upset her," said Flora. "She doesn't want them to know. It would make her hostile if you called there."

"What shall we do, then?" said Mr Foster.

Flora was silent, and Mr Foster waited, but without tension so that she was able to use the silence to think. "Do you like dogs?" she said at last.

"Very much."

"Good. Then will you come for a walk with me, after school tomorrow? I'll introduce you to a really nice golden labrador I know."

· CHAPTER TWENTY-ONE ·

THE CORRIDOR OF light, between the precise moment of school ending and that uncertain time when shadows begin to grow and merge and turn into night, was very narrow by now. Soon it would close altogether and Lisa and Goldie would have to walk along pavements under the reassurance of street lights.

It was cold. The allotments had abandoned all pretence at life and the earth was hard and unreceptive – about as unreceptive as Lisa's mind. She could not prevent Flora, and the tall old man she dimly recognised, walking beside her, especially as he had instantly won Goldie's heart by presenting her with five pink triangular dog biscuits, but she was not willing to listen to what they said. When the old man's red muffler fell away from his neck as he stooped to Goldie's level, revealing that he too wore a dog-collar, she remembered exactly who he was, and was astonished that Flora should have involved him.

The cold burned.

Flora had pulled a woolly hat down over her ears and was holding her scarf up to her mouth with one hand, to warm the air she was breathing. She was aware that the interview was not going well, in fact it was not going at all. Mr Foster had not spoken to anyone but Goldie, and Lisa had not spoken to anyone. Flora thought how very much she would like to turn away and walk home alone.

Then Lisa did say something. "Look," she said abruptly, and she kicked something small and bedraggled into their path – the head of a pigeon. "A fox did that. This is a good year for foxes and crows and all the horrible, evil things."

Flora was shaken at the hostility in her voice. I've left it too late, she thought.

"They're all God's creatures," said Mr Foster mildly. He made a scooping motion with one foot and pushed the partly chewed head out of Goldie's range.

Lisa, her hands forced so hard into her jacket pockets that her fists bulged through the material, was walking ahead, and Flora had to raise her voice to talk to her. "Are you still cross with me about that candle?" she said. "Tell me how a nice smell can possibly be evil."

Lisa ignored her.

"If there's magic in healing herbs," said Flora to Mr Foster, but still talking loudly so that Lisa would hear, "and in colours and scents and energy fields, then God must have put it there. So how can it be wrong to use that magic, as long as you're using it to do good and make people better?"

Mr Foster answered her in his normal voice, not one pitched forward for Lisa's benefit. Flora noticed that Lisa slowed down, just slightly, as he spoke. "It's obviously better to use power for good," he said, "but you do need to be careful. The trick, you see, is to be sure that you acknowledge the power as something that is in the gift of God. Once you believe it's yours, your very own, then you're dancing at the edge of a mighty high cliff. And then, even if you believe you're using the power for good purposes, you're in danger of tipping over."

"Mum thinks she has the power to read the stars," said Flora. "Is she at the edge of the cliff?"

"As I understand it," said Mr Foster, "your mother thinks she has a skill, not a power. Skills, talents, gifts are there to be used – although all or any of them can be misused, of course."

147

Lisa allowed them to catch up with her. "The world is in Satan's power," she said, conscious that in using Barbara's words she had taken on Barbara's tone of voice, but unable to do anything about it. "His magical devices are everywhere, waiting to trap us – and the more innocent they look, the more dangerous they are, because the more likely we are to be deceived by them."

"It might be more helpful," said Mr Foster, "to regard evil as a negative influence, as an absence of light. I understand that some people make the mistake of thinking that a battle for souls is being fought between equal forces. It would be very frightening if that were so, but you see it isn't. Once the light comes, the darkness simply ceases to exist."

Lisa said nothing. She walked, tight-lipped, past the place where her dream had been set; then left the allotments and continued alongside the fence that guarded the dump, Goldie snorting unconcernedly into each tussock of grass as she passed it.

"Lisa," said Mr Foster, suddenly, "do you believe in God?"

"Of course," said Lisa, startled.

"And do you believe that God, who is truth and light and love, wants you to be unhappy and afraid?"

Lisa turned and looked directly at him. He was an academic-looking man, with a serious face that could fall easily into a rather sad expression. She had only ever seen him from a distance before, and he had struck her then as somehow more senior than the headmaster, even a little forbidding.

Now, though, he gazed back at her and said mildly, "I'm just a travelling companion on a walk in the wilderness, Lisa. You're free to ignore me if that's what you prefer."

The three of them stood still, somewhat sheltered by the dump-fence, while Goldie plodded on, unaware she was walking alone.

"Barbara says I mustn't listen to people like you," said Lisa fiercely, "or to Flora."

"Does she say why?" said Mr Foster. He took off his gloves and stuffed them in one coat pocket while he reached for a handkerchief in the other.

For some reason which she didn't understand, it was quite difficult to tell him. She found that she felt rather the way she had felt when Ed had come striding down the road and discovered her in her luminous ghost outfit, rather like that but much more so. "Because," she said, "you've defiled the church with a pagan image."

"Ah," said Mr Foster. He wiped his nose and pushed the handkerchief back into his pocket. "Yes, Flora met him yesterday. He's been welcomed in and blessed, and he's quite at peace with us. He could only defile the church if his influence was the stronger one. I can't think that Mrs Marsh believes the old man to be more powerful than the Almighty!"

"Satan is the prince of this world," said Lisa, her words smoking in the dusky air. "He owns it and everything that's in it."

"Jesus Christ Himself said, 'Now shall the prince of this world be cast out,' " said Mr Foster, quite quietly.

Lisa looked at him.

"The Good Lord made the angels," said Mr Foster, "and gave them free will, as He gave us free will." His eyes were watering with the cold and he rubbed at them with the back of one woollen glove. "But the stories tell that the greatest of the angels became proud, and challenged the power of God, and so fell. He is known by many names; Satan is one of them. At the end, at the day of judgement, redemption is there for him too, if he will take it."

"That's not possible!" said Lisa.

"With God, all things are possible."

Lisa fixed her eyes on Goldie who, realising at last that

149

she had outstripped everyone, had turned and was loping back.

"I would very much like to be able to make you understand," said Mr Foster, "that all that you have glimpsed that is great and good and loving is yours forever, and that all that you have been shown that is frightening and nasty and limiting is yours to reject and forget about."

The long silence that spread through the wintry air was unexpectedly broken by Flora, whose patience had been eroded by cold and anxiety. "And I want you to understand that I'm not some kind of demon just because I tried to buy you a scented candle," she said.

"It isn't just that!" said Lisa. "You know it's more than that."

"What then?" said Flora.

Lisa stared at her. "The tree," she said. But closely though she watched, she didn't catch a glimmer of guilt passing across Flora's face.

"Tree?" said Mr Foster.

"Barbara Marsh and her lot," said Flora, "they've claimed a bit of our garden and they dug up the tree we planted in memory of Mrs Paxton. *And* they dug up everything that was under it. They've taken away Tabitha's mother and her aunt, and they had no right to do that."

Mr Foster raised his eyebrows sharply. "Tabitha is our cat," said Flora, and Mr Foster relaxed his eyebrows again.

"But what do you mean about her mother and her aunt?" said Lisa.

"Mum planted the tree on their grave," said Flora. "Didn't you know? She dug down until she found their bones and then put the roots on top, so they'd feed Mrs Paxton's tree and they'd all go on together."

Lisa stared at her, with a curious expression on her face. "Barbara said she'd found bad things under the tree," she said.

"Oh well," said Flora, "you know what she's like, she

finds what she looks for. Their name things were there, too
– you know, those hollow metal phials you put their address
in? And their amulets."

"Amulets?"

"They each had a little figure of Bast, the Egyptian cat
goddess. It used to hang on their collars, with the name-
tags. If cats are going to wear jewellery at all, they may as
well go for it in a big way!"

The expression on Lisa's face changed twice, first as she
tried not to laugh, and then as she partly gave way to it.
"But why didn't Barbara guess when she saw the collars?"
she said.

"We gave the collars away," said Flora. "It seemed waste-
ful to bury those. But the jewellery was personal – don't
laugh at my cats' mementoes." But she was laughing too.
"Did you really think we'd been conducting ritual sacri-
fices?" she said. "*Did* you?"

Lisa's laugh, though not loud, had got out of control, and
she was beginning to cry.

"I wonder," said Mr Foster, rubbing his woolly-gloved
hands together, "if the air out here isn't a little raw for an
elderly dog?"

"Let's go indoors," said Flora. "We can go to our house,
Mum won't mind. Lisa?"

"All right," said Lisa.

For the first time, she had misjudged the daylight. It was
almost completely dark, and she was as far into bandit-
country as she had ever been. She was glad of company on
the walk back.

As the fence opening loomed ahead, the singing began in
the big house on the other side.

"Who *are* those guys?" said Flora.

"A relatively small group," said Mr Foster. "A break-
away from a larger one. They have strong views and a genuine belief that God in all His glory can be contained within

151

a fixed framework. And they have woken up wonderful things."

"They caused a lot of upset while they did it," said Flora acidly.

"That's how things work, sometimes," said Mr Foster.

As they walked through the fence opening, under the street light, Lisa felt rage explode inside her. "How am I supposed to choose?" she said. "It isn't fair! Barbara says things, you say things . . . How am I supposed to know?"

"When you follow someone," said Mr Foster, "follow consciously, not blindly. We each have to take responsibility for our own actions because when we come to judgement, we'll be judged individually, not *en masse*."

"And what if I get it wrong?"

"That's a risk we all take. Even spiritual leaders can misinterpret the message of God."

"And all the people who've got it wrong," said Lisa, her anger fading as she remembered something awful, "will go to hell-fire? Even the best of them?"

"I find that impossible to believe," said Mr Foster, "but we can safely leave decisions of that magnitude to Heaven. Not everything is our business – and I think you'll find that too much attention paid to hell-fire and Satan gets terribly in the way."

As they reached Katherine's front door, as Flora put her key in the lock, Lisa hesitated, and then turned away. "I have to take Goldie home," she said, so softly they hardly heard her, and catching hold of the dog's collar she walked quickly back down the path. Flora might have tried to stop her, but Mr Foster shook his head.

Lisa shunted Goldie ahead of her into the house and followed her through to the kitchen. The central heating would not come on until her parents got in from work and although it was not cold, it was not very warm either.

Lisa stood in the kitchen, staring down at the table-top but not seeing it, her face without expression.

She could hear the singing quite clearly.

Later, she went out into the dark back garden and stood listening to it. From her position, far enough beyond the reach of the kitchen light to be invisible, she could see into Katherine's kitchen. Katherine, Flora and Mr Foster were sitting round the table in the soft light of an oil lamp. Tabitha was sitting on Mr Foster's lap, and he was scratching the top of her head which was just visible above the table's edge. They looked as if they were in an oil painting.

After a few moments Lisa felt the warm, heavy pressure of Goldie leaning against her leg. "You're a good old girl," she said reaching down to pat her and rub at her wide back. Goldie rocked on her feet with the pressure of the patting and the accompanying wagging of her tail – and her name tag clinked rhythmically against the buckle of her collar.

Lisa stared across Katherine's garden at the new fence and at the space where the hazel tree should have been.

Then she stepped over her own fence. "Come on," she said to the dog, "Flora says you can still hop over if I call you Goldie. Goldie – come on."

Goldie jumped the fence – with some effort, and not without hitting her back feet on the top as she cleared it – and landed with a grunt in Katherine's garden.

Lisa crouched down to put her arms round the dog's neck and kiss the top of her head. Then she stood up and nodded towards Katherine's kitchen door. "Come on," she said, "let's go in to the warm."

Join the RED FOX Reader's Club

The Red Fox Reader's Club is for readers of all ages. All you have to do is ask your local bookseller or librarian for a Red Fox Reader's Club card. As an official Red Fox Reader you only have to borrow or buy eight Red Fox books in order to qualify for your own Red Fox Reader's Clubpack – full of exciting surprises! If you have any difficulty obtaining a Red Fox Reader's Club card please write to: Random House Children's Books Marketing Department, 20 Vauxhall Bridge Road, London SW1V 2SA.

Other great reads ⤐ *from* **Red Fox**

Further Red Fox titles that you might enjoy reading are listed on the following pages. They are available in bookshops or they can be ordered directly from us.

If you would like to order books, please send this form and the money due to:

ARROW BOOKS, BOOKSERVICE BY POST, PO BOX 29, DOUGLAS, ISLE OF MAN, BRITISH ISLES. Please enclose a cheque or postal order made out to Arrow Books Ltd for the amount due, plus 75p per book for postage and packing to a maximum of £7.50, both for orders within the UK. For customers outside the UK, please allow £1.00 per book.

NAME_____

ADDRESS_____

_____

Please print clearly.

Whilst every effort is made to keep prices low, it is sometimes necessary to increase cover prices at short notice. If you are ordering books by post, to save delay it is advisable to phone to confirm the correct price. The number to ring is THE SALES DEPARTMENT 071 (if outside London) 973 9700.

Top teenage fiction from Red Fox

PLAY NIMROD FOR HIM   Jean Ure

Christopher and Nick are each other's only friend.
Isolated from the rest of the crowd, they live in their
own world of writing and music. Enter lively, popular
Sal who tempts Christopher away from Nick . . .
ISBN 0 09 985300 0   £2.99

HAMLET, BANANAS AND ALL THAT JAZZ
Alan Durant

Bert, Jim and their mates vow to live dangerously –
just as Nietzsche said. So starts a post-GCSEs summer
of girls, parties, jazz, drink, fags . . . and tragedy.
ISBN 0 09 997540 8   £3.50

ENOUGH IS TOO MUCH ALREADY
Jan Mark

Maurice, Nina and Nazzer are all re-sitting their
O levels but prefer to spend their time musing over
hilarious previous encounters with strangers, hamsters,
wild parties and Japanese radishes . . .
ISBN 0 09 985310 8   £2.99

BAD PENNY   Allan Frewin Jones

Christmas doesn't look good for Penny this year. She's
veggy, feels overweight, *and* The Lizard, her horrible
father has just turned up. Worse still, Roy appears –
Penny's ex whom she took a year to get over.
ISBN 0 09 985280 2   £2.99

CUTTING LOOSE   Carole Lloyd

Charlie's horoscope says to get back into the swing of
things, but it's not easy: her Dad and Gran aren't
speaking, she's just found out the truth about her
mum, and is having severe confused spells about her
lovelife. It's time to cut loose from all binding ties, and
decide what she wants and who she really is.
ISBN 0 09 91381 X   £3.50